Campfire TALES

TRUE STORIES FROM THE WESTERN FRONTIER

LESTER GALBREATH

BRIGHT SKY PRESS ALBANY, TEXAS

BRIGHT SKY PRESS

Box 416, Albany, Texas 76430

10 9 8 7 6 5 4 3 2 1

Library of Congress Cataloging-in-Publication Data

Galbreath, Lester, 1946–
    Campfire Tales : true stories from the western frontier / by Lester
Galbreath ; illustrations by Charles Shaw.
        p. cm.
    ISBN 1-931721-52-1 (pbk. : alk. paper) 1. Fort Griffin (Tex. : Fort)—History—Anecdotes.
2. Brazos River Valley (Tex.)—History—19th century—Anecdotes. 3. Frontier and pioneer
life—Texas—Brazos River Valley—Anecdotes. 4. Ranch life—Texas—Brazos River Valley—
History—19th century—Anecdotes. 5. Pioneers—Texas—Brazos River Valley—Biography—Anecdotes. 6. Cowboys—
Texas—Brazos River Valley—Biography—Anecdotes. 7. Brazos River Valley (Tex.)—Biography—Anecdotes. 8. Indians
of North America—Texas—Brazos River Valley—History—19th century—Anecdotes. I. Title.

F394.F636G35 2005
976.4—dc22

                                                                              2004063305

Book and cover design by Isabel Lasater Hernandez

Printed in the United States of America

TABLE OF CONTENTS

FOREWORD

his is a collection of a few of the stories I have enjoyed telling over the past thirty-five years. I am in accord with the old saying, "Truth is stranger than fiction," for to me these true stories are more spellbinding and fascinating than any fiction. I have attempted to select tales that allow a glimpse into the lives, dreams and aspirations of those who ventured onto the Texas frontier and settled the Fort Griffin country, and I have endeavored to record the events just as they actually happened.

Many times it is the gunman, the gambler and the outlaw who receive the focus of our attention, but there were also honest, hardworking men and women with a vision for this country. It was the visionaries, not the *pistoleros* and ne'er-do-wells, who stayed and built their dreams. The transients, like the north wind, blew for a while, but then were gone.

CHAPTER 1

THE LAST INDIAN FIGHT

For the most part, Indian reprisals ceased on the Texas frontier after the Battle of Palo Duro Canyon in the fall of 1874. However, there were a few sporadic raids for the next several years, with the last Indian engagement with Fort Griffin soldiers occurring in 1877. In the spring of that year, a small band of Comanche left Indian Territory (in what is now Oklahoma) and returned to the Texas Plains. Captain Phillip L. Lee, commander of Fort Griffin and the nephew of Robert E. Lee, received orders to return them to the reservation—dead or alive. Captain Lee, along with Frank Collinson, a civilian guide, and twenty Tonkawa scouts, took two companies of cavalry, an ambulance, and a doctor and headed for the Staked Plains. Civilian teamsters drove three wagons, two hauling food and bedding for the soldiers, the other hauling grain for the horses. Instead of riding on the wagon seat, the teamsters rode the left-rear mules, driving them with a jerk line and quirt.

They located the Indian trail and followed it in the light that day provided, being then close to Lubbock's present-day location. Chief Johnson, leader of the Tonkawa scouts, believed the Comanche were camping a short distance to the southwest, at Silver Lake, about a three-hour ride from where they were stopping for the night. As they settled into camp, the troopers prepared for battle: Guns were cleaned, tack and gear were checked, and thoughts turned to the possibility of facing a foe that had proven to be both brave and deadly.

Leaving camp the next morning at 3:00 a.m., they gained the Comanche camp near sunrise. Captain Lee divided his forces, sending Company G to approach the village from the south while he led Company I to the north. Suddenly, they heard frantic movements in the camp—the Indians were scrambling for their horses. The cavalry sounded the bugle, and both companies charged. The Comanche chief managed to mount his horse in the melee, pulling an Indian woman up with him and heading for cover. Captain Lee and his company gave chase. First Sergeant Charles Baker was riding an exceptionally fine horse and outdistanced the others to take the lead. As he neared the Indian chief, he shot his carbine—but the gun jammed. His fellow troopers following behind, spurring their horses and pressing to catch up, yelled, "Shoot! Shoot!" Unfortunately, in the excitement and tension of the moment, the sergeant did not think to draw his pistol when the carbine was jammed. In the instant of hesitation, the Indian chief, from horseback, shifted his weight coolly and turned to shoot. He fired one shot—and hit the sergeant squarely in the forehead. Sergeant Baker fell to his death.

The troopers in the rear commenced firing. Then the chief and the woman went down. The battle was quickly over. The Indians, greatly outnumbered, were defeated, but there were significant losses on both sides. Nine Indian warriors and one woman had died, and five women and two children had been captured. The soldiers lost three privates alongside the first sergeant.

That evening, the dead were buried—the Indians placed in a common grave and covered with a wagon sheet, and the three troopers buried side by side, with the first sergeant about six feet in front. The Indian tepees and all other possessions were burned, except those belonging to the five women prisoners. The cavalry returned to Fort Griffin, bringing with them the seven prisoners and their few possessions, as well as twenty-five captured Indian ponies. Later, the five women and two children were returned to the reservation in Indian Territory.

This battle would be Fort Griffin's last Indian battle. For the next three and one-half years, soldiers at Fort Griffin continued to patrol the frontier as Indian activities decreased. Because of the great buffalo hunts conducted by the settlers, the land was not supporting the Indians as it once had. During the peak of the hunts between 1874 and 1878, some eight million buffalo were slaughtered in Texas. Thereafter, the vast buffalo herds were no more, and the Indians' reasons for coming to Texas were greatly diminished. By 1881, there were no Indians living in western Texas. Then, with the buffalo and the Indians gone, the cattlemen could easily drive their cattle into this rich new land.

The settlement of the Texas frontier grew steadily. And by the spring of 1881, the soldiers also marched away for the last time, for Fort Griffin was deemed no longer necessary.

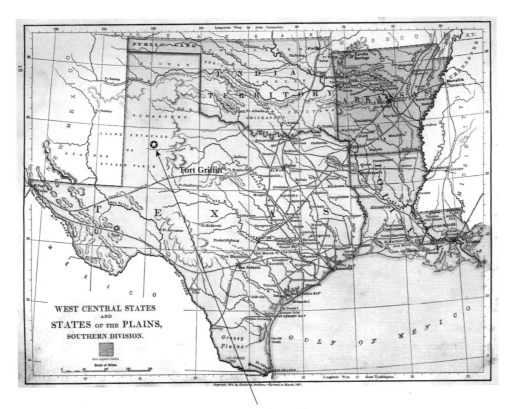

WEST CENTRAL STATES
AND
STATES OF THE PLAINS,
SOUTHERN DIVISION.

Silver Lake—
Site of last Indian engagement
for Fort Griffin troops

CHAPTER 2

BEEHIVE SHOOTOUT

The Beehive Saloon, one of Fort Griffin's most notable saloons, was owned by Owen Donnelly and operated by Mike Forgerty. (Owen Donnelly married Lucinda Selman, sister of John Selman, the Texas gunman who would shoot John Wesley Hardin in an El Paso, Texas, saloon eighteen years later.) It was a two-room adobe building with a saloon in front and a dance hall in the rear. The famous sign swinging over the front door was painted by an artist traveling through Fort Griffin, with a beehive swarming with bees, outlined by honeysuckle. Under the hive was painted this verse:

> In this hive,
> We are all alive:
> Good whiskey makes us funny.
> If you are dry,
> Step in and try
> The flavor of our honey.

In a town like Fort Griffin, there were naturally a number of gunfights in the Beehive. The most deadly, however, occurred on Wednesday, January 17, 1877, between two Fort Griffin lawmen and two cowboys from the Millet ranch, the largest ranch in West Texas at the time. Billy Bland, the Millet ranch foreman, and Charlie Reed, the other Millet cowboy, arrived in town that cold January afternoon and proceeded to get drunk at the Beehive. Before long, they were swearing, yelling, and shooting out the saloon lights—all in good fun.

During the drunken uproar, Dan Barrow, a young lawyer just recently married, came in and bought a pint of whiskey, intending to go straight home. Instead, he became involved in a conversation with another customer and sat down by the front door on the bench against the wall. Another man was sitting at a table in the center of the increasingly raucous room: J. W. Myers, a dishonorably discharged lieutenant from the Tenth Cavalry at Fort Griffin (Buffalo Soldier regiment). Still another customer was Howard W. Peak, a traveling salesman who had just stopped in for a drink. As the shooting started, he ran unhurt out of the saloon to the safety of his hotel.

Word about the volatile situation was quickly sent to Deputy Sheriff William R. Cruger. Cruger took with him William Jeffries, the county attorney, to help arrest Bland and Reed. When the two lawmen arrived, Charlie Reed was standing at the front of the saloon, and Billy Bland was at the rear door leading to the dance hall, taking aim at another light. Bill Cruger advanced toward the rear of the saloon, and Jefferies waited near the front. Cruger told Bland to drop the gun and throw up his hands. Instead, Bland turned on the deputy and fired, wounding Cruger slightly. Instantly, Cruger, Jefferies, Bland, and Reed opened fire on each other.

When the smoke cleared, one man had been killed outright, two were dying from grievous wounds, one had been seriously wounded, one had a flesh wound, and one had escaped unhurt. Dan Barrow, the young lawyer, lay dead on the floor with his brain oozing through a bullet hole in his forehead. He had been hit by one of Charlie Reed's shots. J. W. Myers, the ex-soldier, lay on his side, shot through the back. He died two hours later.

Deputy Sheriff Cruger escaped with only a flesh wound, but Billy Bland was on the floor, writhing on his back and screaming in agony from a gunshot wound to the abdomen. Some townsmen carried him down the street to the Occidental Hotel, where throughout the night, he begged for someone to kill him and put him out of his misery. He died the next morning.

The county attorney William Jefferies had been shot three times; the last shot entered just above his heart and pierced his lung. The other men believed that Mr. Jefferies was dying, so he was taken to the back of the Beehive and placed on a stack of hay. But the next morning, when a cowboy friend came to bury him, he was still alive. The probable reason for his survival was the cold temperature during the night, for the cold had stopped the bleeding. Jeffries did survive, but he was seen the following summer still in a wheelchair. He later practiced law in Albany and then in Colorado City.

That left Charlie Reed, the drunken Millet cowboy. He, oddly enough, had not been hit. When his gun had finally emptied, he had run out the front door toward his horse, which was tied in the Clampett wagon yard. Unfortunately for him, an angry crowd had gathered there, awaiting his return. He felt motivated to leave town on foot and walked the fourteen miles to the Old Stone Ranch, west of Fort Griffin. There he obtained a horse and left the county. Two years later, folks in town heard that he was lynched in Ogallala, Nebraska, for killing a man.

Back then, the town of Fort Griffin rarely noticed dead and dying men. In the aftermath of the Beehive Shootout, music and laughter continued to spill out of the saloons, horses raced up and down the streets, and men kept firing their guns.

HISTORICAL NOTES:

Lieutenant Meyers was dismissed from the army by order of court-martial convened at Fort Griffin on May 27, 1875.

The Millet Ranch was part of a ranching empire owned by several brothers. The oldest brother, Alonzo Millet, ran the ranch north of Fort Griffin. He had the reputation for hiring the toughest men he could find.

The Beehive at one time was owned by the partnership of John (sometimes known as Dick) Shaunessey and Charley Meyers.

CHAPTER 3

MORNING DRINKS

rguments often ended in gunfire or fistfights on the streets of old Fort Griffin, especially between men who considered themselves "bad men." One morning, William A. Martin, better known as Hurricane Bill Martin, and Mike O'Brien were drinking together in the Beehive Saloon and discussing the events of the day. After a number of rounds of red-eye whiskey, both were drunk, and a disagreement grew into a vigorous argument.

After a few more drinks, heated words erupted into action, and both men went for their guns. Suddenly, both realized they were unarmed. Bill sprinted across the street to his shanty for a gun. Mike bolted into the back room of the Beehive and emerged with a buffalo gun. He walked to the middle of the street, sat down in the dirt, and started shooting holes in Bill's house; Bill returned fire through a window.

Soon a small crowd had gathered, some just watching, others cheering for one or the other of the gunmen, offering advice and encouraging them to load faster. One of the onlookers, Bill Campbell, took Mike a drink of whiskey. The men finally ran out of bullets, and by then had forgotten what the argument was even about, so both just got up and went on their separate ways. Neither one had been touched by a bullet.

CHAPTER 4

ONE LONG NIGHT

On a warm afternoon in the 1870s, several cowboys were driving a herd of cattle west of Fort Griffin. Two of the men, Jeff Turner and Smokey, rode ahead in search of water. Like many other men on the Texas frontier, "Smokey" was his nickname, his real name having been discarded for reasons unknown. As they topped a rise, their attention was drawn to movement in the distance. Shading his eyes, Jeff could make out a patch of white. He soon discerned that it was a covered wagon; settlers or traders were venturing out onto the Staked Plains.

As the two men sat watching from their high vantage point, fifteen Indians came into view, traveling in a line that would intersect the wagon's path. The Indians had not as yet discovered the wagon, but if they kept riding in the same direction, they soon would. Smokey and Jeff knew they had to act quickly if the people in the wagon were to live out that afternoon.

Taking a route that would keep them out of the Indians' line of sight, they loped toward the settlers, trying to move noiselessly. They reached the wagon at dusk, and the family—a man, his wife and their small son—had stopped for the night and was settling in to cook supper. Jeff told them about the Indians and pressed them to load the wagon immediately and depart. By the time everything was back in the wagon, it was nearly dark. Abruptly, a shot rang out, and they knew the Indians had found them. Jeff yelled to the man to whip up the mules and make a run for it, while he and Smokey would stay back and try to detain the Indians as long as they could. The two cowboys jumped off their horses and knelt by the only cover available, a few scanty scrub bushes.

Complete darkness swallowed the scene as they pulled their guns, ready to take on the charging Indians. But tense silence prevailed. Each held his breath and strained his ears to hear the approaching Indians, but the lone sound was that of the wagon moving off into the distance. They hunched frozen to the spot. They waited, and their imaginations showed them the Indians getting closer and closer. Their palms began to sweat, and the hair on the back of their necks stood up. As they waited in the darkness, their minds told them to hold their ground and fight, but their feet demanded to run! Their feet won the argument, and they jumped up to flee. As they did, the Indians jumped up off the ground all around them, bullets and arrows flying. In the darkness and confusion, they broke through the enemy lines without a scratch, bursting out the other side at a dead run.

They weren't sure where they were or where they were going, but any place was better than where they'd been. Suddenly, the ground just dropped out from under them; they had run off the edge of a steep ravine. They fell, hit the rocky walls, rolled, fell again, slid hard, fell a few more feet, and finally landed with a thud. They managed to get to their feet and, after taking stock of their faculties, they found only scratches and bruises, no broken bones. When they looked up, they could see at the top edges of the ravine some sky that was still lighted against the darker night sky. They saw that to the south the sky was lighter and to the north it was very dark. They knew, then, that the mouth of the canyon was to the south, so they started down the ravine in that direction. Soon they perceived moving shadows to the south and knew that the Indians had entered the canyon and were coming towards them.

Turning in that instant to the north, they walked until they came up against a solid rock wall. It was too dark to see, so they urgently felt along the rock with their hands, trying to find something to grip, to begin a climb out of the ravine. Finding nothing, Jeff told Smokey to stand on his shoulders so he could reach higher. As Jeff eased along the bluff allowing Smokey's hands to scrabble for any escape hold, Smokey suddenly said, "Wait! There's a little hole up here." Jeff pushed while Smokey stretched and clawed along, finally managing to climb into a small opening that he hoped was a cave. The roof was very low, with only enough room for sitting. Smokey reached down and helped Jeff climb in. They wanted to get as far in as possible, for if the Indians found them in that little hole, they would be sitting ducks. The roof was too low for them to walk, but they could crawl on their hands and knees.

At first they had believed this hole was just a small cave, so they were surprised that they could keep crawling in deeper and deeper. Eventually, they realized they could no longer feel the walls or the roof, so they slowly stood up. It was as their knees straightened that there came a loud buzzing. Everyone on the Texas frontier dreaded that sound! They froze, afraid to move. Jeff had two matches, and he struck one. In the flickering light, they could see that they were in a large room, and thousands of rattlesnakes were covering the floor—great balls of snakes unwinding and slithering in all directions. The match went out, and in the darkness they could hear—they could feel!—the snakes on all sides. Hurriedly, Jeff lit the other match. The snakes were becoming more agitated, buzzing louder and louder. Then, that last match went out. Anyone who's ever been in a deep cave knows that the darkness in a cave is the blackest black ever seen. Jeff and Smokey strained every muscle in their bodies, trying not to move, not even to breathe, until finally they eased into a sitting position back to back, leaning against each other. With every animal instinct they wanted to run, but they did not know the way to the tunnel leading out.

After a while, Jeff started talking. He told Smokey that Indians had killed his wife and children several years before. He went on to say that if his time to die had come, he was ready. Suddenly, Jeff jerked, then told Smokey he had been bitten. Soon Jeff was thrashing about in great pain, talking wildly. Smokey tried to hold him, offering comfort while trying not to disturb the snakes. After a long time Jeff became still, and Smokey knew that he had died.

Sitting in the darkness alone, Smokey endured through the terrifying night. After a long time, something strange appeared. It took a moment for Smokey's eyes to focus on the small beam of light in the distance. At first, he could not comprehend what he was seeing. Finally, he realized it must be morning, and sunlight was shining through the entry tunnel. He had not heard the snakes for some time, and he did not know where they were. One thing was sure, though: He was leaving this tomb, no matter what. Crawling along and dragging Jeff's body, he reached the outside without encountering a snake. He lowered Jeff's body down the face of the bluff to the ground, then jumped.

The morning sky revealed Indian tracks on the ground but no Indians in sight. Walking out of the ravine, he came upon the wagon and the family from the night before. They were cooking breakfast and told Smokey that a troop of cavalry returning to Fort Griffin had heard the attack and rushed to their rescue. The Indians, having decided that discretion was the better part of valor, had departed.

Smokey sat down to eat breakfast with the family, and to rest.

Before he had spent the night in the cave, Smokey had had black hair, but when he left the cave, his hair was snow white.

HISTORICAL NOTE:

Along the sandy bottom of that canyon, it is thought that Smokey probably buried Jeff Turner in a shallow grave dug out with his hunting knife.

CHAPTER 5

A SURPRISE VISITOR

Wild Indians were not the only danger on the Texas frontier of the 1870s. John Selman and his wife, Edna, lived about nine miles up the Clear Fork River from Fort Griffin. One evening in 1875, a Mr. Webb was visiting in the Selman home. He and John sat talking in the front room of the house, Edna was boiling coffee in the kitchen, and their son William, an infant of only a few months, slumbered on a bed in the front room. Suddenly, John's dogs started barking and quickly became very agitated, barking more and more urgently. John became worried—someone or something was outside the house. He opened the door to look outside and barely got out of the way as one of the dogs charged into the house. Right on the dog's tail, snarling and growling, was a large mountain lion. Everyone was stunned and, for a bare instant, frozen in place. The wildcat jumped onto the bed, its jaws closed on little William, and it tensed to spring for the door. John, not wanting the wildcat to get outside with the baby, slammed the door shut. The fireplace was behind him, with a small stack of wood beside it. John grabbed a stick of firewood and, swinging it with both hands, smote the mountain lion. Dazed, the cat dropped little William, and Edna ran to pick him up. Striking back, the wildcat clawed Edna, leaving deep gashes on her face and breast.

Mr. Webb finally collected his wits, grabbed the lion by the tail and flung it into the fireplace. A fire was burning, and the cat leaped out, throwing hot coals across the room. It ran under the bed. John crossed the room and got his double-barreled shotgun. Cocking both hammers, he stuck it under the bed and pulled *both* triggers. As they say, the wildcat gave up the ghost. Edna carried the scars the rest of her life, and William was always hard of hearing in his left ear.

CHAPTER 6

COMANCHE RAID, 1867

In the spring of 1867, eighteen Comanche rode out of Indian Territory for a raid into Texas. The frontier was still unprotected, as the federal military was trying to recover from the Civil War that had just ended two years before. Only later that year were forts manned along the western settlements with the establishment of Fort Griffin, Fort Sill, and Fort Richardson. The Indians swept through the counties of Shackelford and Stephens, successfully stealing a number of horses. These hard riding Indians usually struck swiftly in Texas and then disappeared back into the Indian Territory. This time, as soon as they had gathered a herd of horses, they headed north. As they passed near the J. C. Lynch ranch, they stopped long enough to kill and scalp a settler's young daughter. They then traveled several miles and camped on Foyle Creek near its confluence with the Brazos River's Clear Fork, located about four miles east of where Fort Griffin would be built three months later.

Their camp was situated in brush and not visible from any distance. In the evening, the Indians spotted two cowboys, Arch Ratcliff and Andy McDonald, riding across the prairie. The Comanche knew that cowboys naturally checked brands on loose livestock, so they devised a good idea for an ambush. They hurriedly led a horse out and hobbled him as a decoy, while they hid in the thicket along the creek bank. Sure enough, seeing the loose horse, the cowboys rode into the ambush when trying to check the brand. As soon as the two men were near, the Indians opened fire. Andy and Arch returned a volley, but realizing they were greatly outnumbered, they pulled their horses around, raised a dust cloud getting out of there, and headed down the Clear Fork to sound the alarm. Surprisingly, no one on either side was hit.

By the next morning, eighteen men were ready to fight the Indians. They picked up the trail on the north side of the river and followed it about twenty miles. They overtook the Indians on Mule Creek, near where Haskell is located today. A heated fight ensued, but in the end the settlers were forced to retreat. One man, John Glen, was slightly injured, and no Indians were killed. Regrouping a short distance from the fight, and after some discussion, they decided to return home for the time being.

About ten days later, they were still determined to teach the Indians a lesson. T. E. Jackson, whose stone ranch house is now the Fort Griffin State Park residence, called for volunteers. Eight men responded: W. D. Reynolds, George Reynolds, John Anderson, Nelson Spears, Andy McDonald, Si Hough, Jim Derky, and Elsy Christianson, with T. E. Jackson being elected captain of the expedition. The party was heavily armed, well supplied, and mounted on good horses. They traveled about forty miles northwest to what is now the location of Aspermont.

As they neared the Double Mountain Fork of the Brazos River, a dust cloud was seen in the distance, and upon inspection they discovered a running herd of buffalo. Spurring their horses, they were soon close enough to see that the herd was being chased by a band of Indians. The Jackson group stopped a few minutes for a brief council of war. They decided that the best plan was to circle around the Indians while staying out of sight in the foothills along a creek. The plan worked so well that they took the Indians completely by surprise. When they came out of the brush on their side of the river, they found one Indian skinning a buffalo. Jackson's group opened fire, and the Indian tried desperately to catch his frightened horse. When the horse broke away, he turned to face the oncoming cowboys and return fire. He faced his enemies bravely, but he soon went down from several shots.

Across the river, hidden from view by the tree line were six Indians. With the outbreak of gunfire, they charged, but one of their number was killed as they came up the river bank. As he fell, the others halted, and a heated battle erupted. Both sides knew it was a fight to the finish. After an exchange of several volleys of fire, the Jackson men charged, and the Indians were pushed back. Then, knowing it would terrorize their foes, the white men scalped the two dead Indians as the others watched.

The five remaining Indians broke and ran for their lives. Captain Jackson and his men gave chase, and their grain-fed horses proved to be stronger and faster than the grass-fed horses of the Indians. Several times the Indians tried to cross an open prairie to the rough breaks on the opposite side, but the settlers managed to turn them back. The running battle had covered two miles when Jackson's band caught up with the Indians.

George Reynolds and Andy McDonald were riding side by side directly behind the Indians. One of the Indians turned on his running horse and took aim with his bow. George, believing the Indian was shooting at Andy, yelled, "Watch out, Andy!" But the arrow hit George, bouncing off a U. S. cavalry belt buckle he was wearing before entering his body just above the navel. When he pulled the shaft out, the metal arrowhead remained in his body. Si Hough, riding off to the side, saw George hit, and in a fury yelled, "I'm getting his scalp!" Running the Indian down, Si shot him, and, true to his word, he scalped him.

Meanwhile, George Reynolds was in great pain and forced to dismount. T. E. Jackson stayed with him while the rest of the group continued the fight. Very soon, they had shot and scalped the remainder of the Indians, except one who made his escape through the rough thicket along the river.

The battle finally over by sundown, they now had to get George some medical help. The men tied two horses together, head and tail, and laying George on a pack in between, started the long, slow journey home. Two other men had received wounds: John Anderson had received a painful arrow wound in his left wrist, and a Minié ball had gone through the sleeve into the arm of Will Reynolds. While the rest of the men slowly guided the horses carrying George, John and Will went ahead, riding all night for help. Will later told of the eerie feeling they had as they rode through thousands of stampeding buffalo that dark night.

The two men arrived at the Reynolds' home known as "Old Stone Ranch" the next day about noon. Sam Newcomb, brother-in-law of George and Will Reynolds, saddled his best horse and rode one hundred miles to Weatherford for a doctor, stopping only as necessary at ranches along the way to trade for a fresh horse. He then made the return trip with Dr. James D. Ray, arriving at Old Stone Ranch shortly after Captain Jackson and the rest of the men arrived.

It had been a long and painful trip for George, but he had endured, despite being seriously wounded. Dr. Ray probed the wound but was unable to locate the arrowhead. In time the wound healed, and though he never complained, George suffered pain from the metal spike for the next fifteen years.

Years later, a knot appeared near his spine. Suspecting it might be the arrowhead, he sought medical help in Kansas City. The following excerpt from the *Kansas City Journal* dated July 18, 1882, describes the incident.

Yesterday afternoon there was removed from the body of George T. Reynolds, a prominent cattleman of Fort Griffin, Texas, an arrowhead, two inches long. Mr. Reynolds had carried this head sixteen years, three months, and fifteen days.

On Friday last the gentleman came to this city and registered at the St. James hotel. His coming was for the purpose of having a surgical operation performed.

On his back opposite the place where the arrow entered his body, he could feel its head. At last he decided to have it cut out and came to Kansas City as mentioned. Scales of rust were removed from the arrowhead when it was taken from his body. The point was blunt, as if it had been eaten off with rust. This operation was performed by Drs. Lewis and Griffith, in the presence of Dr. Powell of New York. The gentleman was resting easy last evening and feeling much relieved.

These were the days before anesthesia, and George would not allow the doctor to proceed unless he promised to stop when George asked him to. Two friends accompanied George into the surgery room. As soon as the doctor started cutting, one friend hastened to make an exit. The other, "Shanghai" Pierce, stayed with his friend. But when the doctor made a deep incision, Shanghai became excited and yelled, "You're cutting him to the hollow!" George said, *Stop!* and sat up. As he leaned forward, the arrowhead popped out.

George Reynolds' sister, Sallie Ann Reynolds Matthews, later wrote concerning the Indians being scalped, "There were several scalps, scalps not taken in wanton cruelty, but as a lesson to the Indians." It seems the frontiersmen intended to demoralize the Indians by using their own tactics against them.

HISTORICAL NOTES:

The Old Stone Ranch house was built in 1856 and, at that time, was the last house between the Texas frontier and Santa Fe as settlers headed west.

The metal arrowhead, probably made from a discarded barrel ring, removed from George Reynolds is still in the possession of his family.

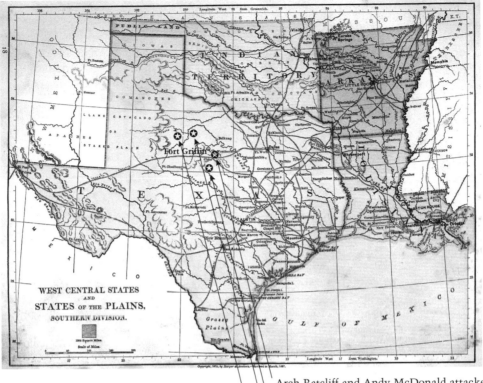

Fort Griffin

Arch Ratcliff and Andy McDonald attacked

Girl scalped and killed

Site of first Indian battle

Site of second Indian battle—George Reynolds wounded

CHAPTER 7

ELM CREEK RAID

The year was 1864 and, while the country was locked in civil war, the Plains Indians were renewing their efforts to take back a portion of the Texas frontier. Settlers who were trying to live along Elm Creek on the outermost reaches of the frontier found themselves appallingly vulnerable to Indian raids. Three years later, Fort Griffin would be built twenty-five miles southwest of these settlements, but that would occur after one of the bloodiest raids in the annals of the Texas-Indian wars.

On Thursday morning, October 13, 1864, about 11:00, the people living near Elm Creek in north-central Texas saw the first smoke signal, but by then it was too late to prepare any defense. Frenzied hordes of Indians struck with full fury, and the carnage lasted all day. Chief Little Buffalo led seven hundred Comanche and Kiowa braves in the attack. A number of people lost their lives that day, and for others the physical pain and mental anguish devastated their lives for many years.

Peter Harmonson and his son Perry were the first to spot the Indians hunting cattle on Rabbit Creek. As the Indians rode into view, Peter wasted no time and shot the lead Indian; then, spinning their horses around, he and Perry raced through the thickets along the creek. Mr. Harmonson still had a wounded left arm from an Indian fight that had occurred a few miles east, where he and five other men had been attacked by thirty Comanche just a month before. Two of his friends had been killed, and he had barely escaped with his life. Now, he and his son made a mad dash for the safety of nearby Fort Murrah, a small outpost that had recently been established by the Texas Rangers in an attempt to help protect this part of Texas. The Harmonsons reached Murrah unharmed but were dismayed to find that most of the Rangers were away on a scouting expedition. Many who would later hear reports of the vicious raid on Elm Creek would conclude that the Indians had been scouting that exact area, for they were able to plan the attack on a day when most of the men were away from home.

The Indians crossed the Brazos River. Spying Joel Miers, they killed and scalped him. Continuing south toward Elm Creek, they encountered seven Rangers returning to Fort Murrah. After a short, heated battle, six of the Rangers were killed, with Lieutenant Carson alone escaping. Carson made it to the post and confirmed Harmonson's story: The country was beset by raging Indians. Mr. Harmonson and another gentleman climbed on the roof of a post building and, with a spyglass, searched the surrounding area. Across the river about a mile and half away, they witnessed Indians attacking the McCoy place and, even as they watched, saw James McCoy and his seventeen-year-old son slain. Several Rangers charged across that space of prairie and managed to save Mrs. McCoy and her niece, Betty Morris, and delivered them to safety at the fort.

William George Wooten discovered Indians approaching his cabin. Grabbing a double-barreled shotgun, he jumped on his horse and rode for his life. One attacking Comanche chased Wooten, while the others raced to other settlers' homes. Gaining ground, the Comanche opened fire, shooting Wooten's horse from under him. Wooten jumped free and hit the ground running. The Indian had known him at Camp Cooper a few years earlier and thought it funny to watch Wooten running as hard as he could, ripping and tearing his clothes on the underbrush. The wily Indian stayed just out of shotgun range and laughingly taunted, "Run, Wooten! Run! Run, Wooten! Run!" Enjoying the chase, the Indian got a little too close, for Wooten was able to whirl around and shoot him with a load of buckshot. By then, Wooten's clothes were in rags, and all he had left were his shirt and long johns. But he did escape with his life.

Splitting into several large groups, the swarm of Indians raced to terrorize everyone they could find. Hearing shots, Thomas Hamby concealed his family in the cliffs near their home. He and his son, Thornton, had arrived home on leave from the Confederate army just days before. Quickly saddling their horses, they sped to warn a neighbor, Dr. Thomas J. Wilson, who hurried to hide his family down their well, shoving a large rock over the top. He then accompanied the Hambys to spread the alarm.

Flying past the Harry D. Williams home, the Hambys and Dr. Wilson shouted, "Run for the brush and hide! Indians are coming! Indians! Indians!" All the men were away from home, but there were five ladies and several children at the house. Mrs. Williams rushed them all to the creek bottom to hide in the wild plum and briar thickets. As they slid down the bank of Elm Creek, Mrs. John Stanley's long braid became caught on a tree limb, and she was suspended, unable to free herself. Mrs. Williams scrambled back up the bank, pulled a knife from her skirt, and cut the braid from Mrs. Stanley's head. There were several acts of heroism that desperate day, and Mrs. Williams was certainly a heroine as she maintained her calm and kept these women and children quiet and hidden all day.

The Hambys and Dr. Wilson were in an all-out race for their lives as they were now involved in a running gun battle with the Indians. They at last found refuge at the George Bragg ranch, where twenty-five people in the main house were able to mount a substantial defense. George's sister-in-law, Mary Bragg, lived on an adjoining ranch and was cut off as she and her two small children tried to get to the safety of her brother-in-law's home. Her husband, Billy, was away on a trip to Weatherford. Mary survived by hiding with her children under a rock ledge on the creek. Several times during the day Indians passed close by, and she exercised all her courage to keep the children quiet and still. Their dog had followed, but he, too, seemed sensible of the danger and made not a sound. The long, terrifying hours slowly ticked by for the small, huddled group, but they remained undetected.

The battle around the Bragg ranch house raged for six hours. The people forted up there included the Hambys and Dr. Wilson, George Bragg and his family, Mrs. Alfred Foster and her four children, Nathan Bragg and family, Martin B. Bragg and family, Sol Bragg, and Britt Johnson's daughter, Eliza Bragg. Several of the defenders were wounded, but there was only one casualty—Dr. Wilson was shot through his heart by an arrow as he stood at his place of defense before a window. An estimated twenty to twenty-five Indians were killed in the Elm Creek Raid , most of those during the siege at the Bragg house, including Chief Little Buffalo, who was killed by a large-bore gun.

As the Braggs fought for their lives, Indians had fanned out three miles along the residences near Elm Creek, attacking every living person in sight. The last residence to be attacked that day was the two-story Carter house. As was true at several of the other houses, only women were at home. As the Indians charged around the house with demoniac war whoops, twenty-one-year-old Milly Durkin frantically bolted and locked the doors and shutters. Inside the house with Milly were her family members: her five-year-old daughter Elizabeth (called "Lottie"); her twenty-eight-month-old daughter Milly Jane; an unnamed infant son; her mother, Mrs. Elizabeth FitzPatrick; and Elijah Carter, her ailing thirteen-year-old brother. Also in the Carter house were: Mary Johnson, the pregnant wife of Britt Johnson; her five-year-old son; her seven-year-old son; and a daughter of four years.

Milly Durkin hid her infant son under the bed and armed herself with a rifle, determined to protect her children if it were within her power. Several Indian braves broke down the front door with their tomahawks, while Milly was firing through the door as fast as she was able to reload. With the heart of a lioness, she defended her family until she was overcome by the furious Indians. She was dragged outside and bludgeoned to death by the warriors' tomahawks. Her mother was held by other braves and caused to watch while Milly's skull was bashed in and she was scalped. Jim, one of the small Johnson boys, tried to run but was caught near the front yard gate and killed. Milly's unnamed baby boy was found under the bed and repeatedly thrown against the wall until he was dead. The others were taken captive. It was now nearly dark, and, securely tying their hostages on horses, the Indians rode off into the night, leaving death, destruction, and broken lives behind.

They rode into a north wind all night and all the next day without stopping. They pushed on through the moonlight of the second night, not stopping for any length of time until Saturday morning. As the dust of Thursday's action still hung in the air, the settlers from Elm Creek had acted to mount a rescue. But the hard-riding Indians had vanished into the Texas wilderness. By the time the Indians finally stopped, Elijah Carter, the young son of Elizabeth FitzPatrick, had become too sick from drinking gypsum water to travel farther—or even to sit upright. The raiders gathered brush into a pile, tied the thirteen-year-old boy on top, and forced his mother to watch while they set it afire. Mrs. FitzPatrick now witnessed the second horrifying death of her only two children at the hands of these Indians: Her daughter Milly had been tomahawked, and now she suffered Elijah's screams as he was burned alive.

After the Elm Creek Raid, Britt Johnson made several trips into Indian territory looking for his family. Searching eight months, he finally located his wife and children and managed to ransom them back. Many other settlers and their children did not fare as well. The child Milly Jane Durkin was reported by the Indians to have died from starvation and exposure, and all official reports concluded that she, indeed, was dead. Elizabeth FitzPatrick remained with the Indians for two years until Colonel Leavenworth found her as an Indian slave near Fort Dodge, Kansas. After being rescued, she returned to Texas and settled in Parker County near Weatherford. Young Lottie Durkin was found with Chief Silver Broach's band in Kansas and was reunited with her grandmother, Elizabeth FitzPatrick, in Weatherford. Elizabeth FitzPatrick, after marrying her fourth husband, Isaiah Clifton, moved with him and Lottie to Fort Griffin. The Cliftons lived the rest of their lives there and are buried in the main cemetery at Fort Griffin.

Faring better than most, Billy and Mary Bragg also moved to Fort Griffin after the raid, and Mr. Bragg became known affectionately as Uncle Billy Bragg. Lottie Durkin married Dave Barker, a Fort Griffin deputy sheriff, but never fully recovered from her ordeal with the Indians; after moving to Old Tascosa with her husband, she died at the young age of twenty-eight.

HISTORICAL NOTES:

Mary and Britt Johnson were a black family, and Britt had the reputation of being one of the best rifle shots in Texas. He made several trips into Indian Territory, attempting to rescue his family. The movie *The Searchers*, with John Wayne, was taken from Britt's story. Four years after Britt succeeded in finding his family, he was killed by Indians about forty miles northeast of Fort Griffin on Turtle Creek.

During Lottie Durkin's captivity the Indians tattooed a blue half-moon on her forehead, which she had for the rest of her life.

Camp Cooper was a federal military pre-Civil War post on the Clear Fork of the Brazos River, nine miles north of where Fort Griffin would be built after the Civil War, when the United States re-established its western line of defense. Robert E. Lee was commander there of the two squadrons of the Second Cavalry for nineteen months, beginning on April 9, 1856.

CHAPTER 8

TRUE STORIES FROM THE WESTERN FRONTIER

TWENTY TO ONE

In the summer of 1860 the Second Cavalry stationed at Camp Cooper spent most of their time in the saddle. Protecting the Texas frontier in the days when the Comanche and Kiowa roamed the Clear Fork country was a full-time job.

On August 25, Major George H. Thomas led a patrol of a Company D detachment under Lieutenant Lowe, augmented by members of the regimental band, to scout through present-day Taylor County. That patrol located a fresh Indian trail. With the assistance of Doss, their Delaware Indian guide, the cavalrymen followed the trail until nightfall. Early on the morning of the 26th, Major Thomas resumed the trail, and by 7:00 a.m. Doss had discovered a band of thirteen Indians breaking camp on the Salt Fork of the Brazos River. As soon as Thomas received the scout's report, he ordered the company forward at the gallop. They entered the campsite only minutes after the Comanche had departed, and hurrying on, they soon closed to within sight of the fleeing Indians.

An all-out running battle began and continued for the next three miles. The soldiers pressed the Indians so closely that they abandoned their loose horses. The situation soon became desperate for the Indians. Suddenly, one old Comanche warrior reined up his horse and slid to the ground. Armed only with bow and arrows and his lance, he defiantly faced his enemies.

The soldiers rushed to dispatch the lone brave, but this old warrior had survived many battles during his life, and that day he fought with the heart of a young tiger. He hit Major Thomas with glancing blows by two arrows, one to his chin and the other in his chest. Neither caused a serious wound, but both left deep cuts. The Comanche also managed to kill trooper William Murphy and wound bandsmen John Zito and Casper Siddel with well-placed arrows. After being shot twenty or more times, he still lanced and wounded trooper Hugh Clark and bugler August Hausser. Finally, the old warrior fell, mortally wounded. He had lost his personal battle, but he had bought enough time for the rest of his band to escape. Major Thomas treated the wounded of his detachment, and with twenty-eight captured Indian ponies, the troops returned to Camp Cooper in a pouring rainstorm.

Major George H. Thomas became a famous Civil War commander, earning the nickname "Rock of Chickamauga." During all the years of his army life—through the Indian wars, the Civil War, the Second Seminole and Mexican wars—he was only wounded twice, those being the same wounds received from the old Comanche warrior on the Texas frontier near Camp Cooper, August 26, 1860.

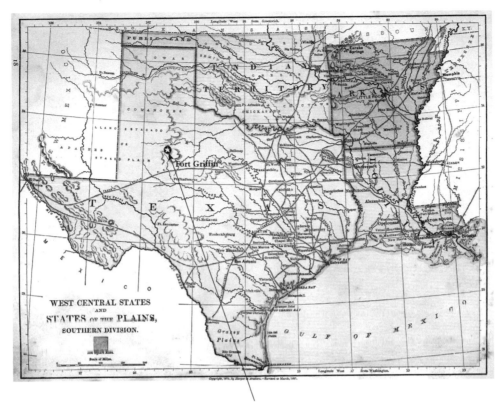

Site of Comanche battle

CHAPTER 9

WHISTLING SAM

Fort Griffin was established in early summer, 1867, and by the fall of that year Samuel and Susan Newcomb built their home about a mile west on Collins Creek. Sam, an enterprising young man, selected a spot between the fort and the river to open a mercantile store, apparently becoming the first merchant in the new town of Fort Griffin. Other merchants and speculators would follow his lead, and Fort Griffin in a score of years would grow into one of the most notable and busy towns on the frontier. This county was still wild and largely unsettled, and the men—and some of the ladies—routinely carried guns. It was not unusual for the men to have one or two pistols in their belts and a rifle close at hand.

Like most frontier settlements, Fort Griffin at this early date had not as yet built a church, nor was there a regular minister. A circuit-riding preacher did visit from time to time, and on those occasions he held services in someone's home, with neighbors from several miles around attending. For a time Reverend Clark, a Baptist preacher from Weatherford, made the trip once a month, but he always walked the one hundred miles, believing there was less danger from Indians if he had no horse to steal.

On one such evening's occasion, when Reverend Clark was holding services in town, Sam and Susan Newcomb decided to walk the mile to church with their small son, Gus. Instead of hitching the buckboard, they enjoyed a leisurely stroll on a warm, clear evening. After church, Gus' grandparents, Mr. and Mrs. Barber Watkins Reynolds, wanted to have their grandson go home to Reynolds Bend with them for a visit. So Gus left with the older folks, and Samuel and his wife walked home in the moonlight.

Suddenly, as they walked along talking quietly, Sam discerned movement up ahead. They stopped breathlessly, hearts hammering, when they realized it was ten Indians riding single file *directly toward them.* With horror, they discovered in that moment that their guns had been left at home, there was no place to hide, and they surely could not outrun the mounted warriors.

Death, they both knew, was imminent. Yet, in that instant of peril, for some reason he could never explain afterwards, Sam started whistling. Surprised, the Indians reined up their horses and sat, staring intently at the couple. Sam's and Susan's hearts beat audibly, and seconds ticked by for what seemed like hours. Incredibly, the Indians did gather their reins and urge their horses forward but then, inexplicably, turned from the trail and rode off.

Why did they leave? Why had they not attacked? Did Sam's whistling have anything to do with their leaving? No one knows. Maybe because the fort was so close, the Indians thought it was a signal to the soldiers.

It was dark and difficult for the Newcombs to see if the Indians had really left or were still near. They hurried on home, where Sam was faced with a dilemma: Should he take Susan with him as he went for help, or would she be safer in the cabin? He well knew that if the couple was caught out in the open, their chances of survival would not be good. On the other hand, Sam reasoned, Susan could lock the doors and windows, and if the Indians did attack, he would have returned with reinforcements before they could break in.

Not wanting to draw attention to the house, they knew it was best not to light the lamps. So Susan waited in the dark, while Sam saddled his horse and rode to the fort for help. Sam returned with the soldiers, who searched the area carefully—to find the Indians gone!

There were many uncertainties and dangers along the Clear Fork River in those early days, such as wild animals, disease, or injury. These dangers were much more serious in such a settlement than they are today because the doctor was either unavailable or located far away. And, there were many instances on the frontier when sudden encounters with native nomads turned deadly. But on this day, two young pioneers had faced the dangers of settling a new land and had lived to tell the tale. A sad thing happened to them later, though: After surviving the Indians, even though unarmed, Samuel Newcomb died at the young age of thirty—from the measles.

HISTORICAL NOTE:

Mr. and Mrs. Barber Watkins Reynolds were the parents of Susan Reynolds Newcomb and the maternal grandparents of Watt Matthews of Lambshead Ranch.

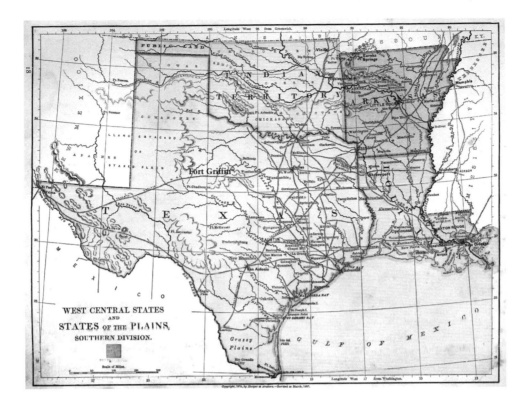

WEST CENTRAL STATES
AND
STATES OF THE PLAINS,
SOUTHERN DIVISION.

Scale of Miles.

CHAPTER 10

THE CHIEF OF RED MUD

In the early 1870s, a band of outlaws was operating out of Blanco Canyon near an area called Red Mud, which today is found in Dickens County. Charlie Smith, the leader of the gang, assumed the nickname "The Chief of Red Mud" and was not only a self-proclaimed bad man but supposedly the toughest man in that band of cutthroats. One day, the Chief of Red Mud rode into Fort Griffin (or The Flat, as it was sometimes called), proceeded to the nearest saloon and drank his way through town. As his consumption of firewater grew, so did his boast of being a *bad man.*

That day, the sheriff and his deputies were out of town on the trail of horse thieves. While the Chief was usually viewed as only a bully and braggart, he also had the reputation of being ruthless. So, no one in town wanted to press the issue, and everyone was satisfied to just stay out of his way. For a while he paraded up the street and down, firing his guns to emphasize his swagger and boasting. He made quite an imposing figure—with two Colt 45s and a Bowie knife in his belt.

When locomoting down the street from the Beehive Saloon, the Chief had the notion to take charge of the Charlie Meyer Saloon, where Jules Hurvey, an ex-circus man, was the barkeeper. Jules was determined not to give ground to the bully, and he contrived to "take the bull by the horns." Retrieving a rope from a peg on the wall, he spread a loop on the floor. When the Chief stepped in, he pulled the noose tight around his legs and jerked his feet from under him. The Chief hit the floor hard; his guns jarred from his hands and slid across the floor. Before his stunned and drunken senses could be collected, Jules pulled the rope through a hammock ring on the wall and hoisted Charlie up until his hands could just touch the floor.

The mighty Chief of Red Mud bellowed like a raging bull, threatening everyone in hearing. But Jules leaned out the door and announced in his best circus voice, "Come in and see the wild animal!" A small crowd gathered and delighted in poking fun at the terror of The Flat. Hanging upside down is not very comfortable anytime, but hanging upside down while drunk can be a nightmare. Charlie Smith's bravado was soon reduced to begging for mercy.

Finally, Jules loosened the rope and let him down. Charlie managed to right himself on unsteady legs, exit the saloon to mount his horse, and ride on out of Fort Griffin. The fearsome Chief of Red Mud returned to the Texas plains and his shady dealings, occasionally stealing horses and cattle. But, his days as a town-tamer—especially at Fort Griffin—were over.

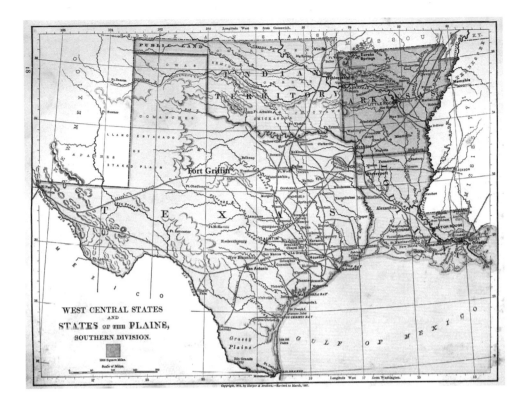

WEST CENTRAL STATES
AND
STATES OF THE PLAINS,
SOUTHERN DIVISION.

CHAPTER 11

THE PRICE OF TOBACCO

The military stationed at Fort Griffin included contingents of cavalry and infantry. The cavalry required large numbers of horses, and remounts were normally not easy to acquire. As the town of Fort Griffin grew, outlaws and horse thieves became a daily fact of life. The post commander was concerned that cavalry horses ridden to town and left in front of stores and saloons would turn up missing. Therefore, he issued a special order: "Horses are not to be ridden to town."

Early one Sunday morning, a trooper working his horse behind the mess halls discovered he was out of tobacco. He rode up to the sutler's store on the garrison, but they had none. Now he had three choices: one, do without; two, walk to town; or three, *ride his horse* to town. He knew that if he violated the order prohibiting taking a horse into town, and was caught, he would be in serious trouble. It was early, and there was not much activity on the post. The town would certainly still be asleep, for it was always wild and woolly until almost dawn on Saturday nights. The more he thought about it, the more it seemed harmless to go straight to town, get a plug of tobacco, and come straight back. So, he and his horse trotted down to the first store in town.

Once at the store, it occurred to him to worry that he may have made a mistake if, by chance, something should happen to his horse. Well, he did not want to think about *that*. Just to make sure the horse was safe, he snapped his twenty-eight-foot picket rope to the horse halter and took a firm grip on the other end while he went into the store.

It took only a minute to buy the tobacco and come back out onto the street. But his heart nearly stopped beating when he saw that there was nothing—not a thing!—on the other end of his picket rope: His horse was gone! Someone had cut the rope and ridden off on *his horse.*

Frantically, he searched everywhere, but to no avail. He considered deserting, as disobeying an order meant serious punishment—possibly a dishonorable discharge.

Finally, he just returned to the post to face the music. After some thought, the post commander decided on the punishment: The trooper was to stand on the head of a barrel from colors to colors for three days with one hour off for lunch.

HISTORICAL NOTES:

A picket rope was a rope with a picket pin that cavalrymen carried with them. The metal pin was driven into the ground, while the horse was tied to it with the twenty-eight-foot rope and allowed to graze.

The phrase "colors to colors" referred to the flag being put up at 6:00 each morning and taken down at 6:00 each night.

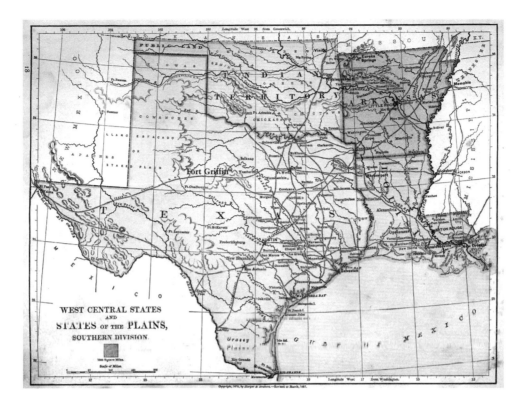

WEST CENTRAL STATES
AND
STATES OF THE PLAINS,
SOUTHERN DIVISION

CHAPTER 12

THE LEE FAMILY MASSACRE

In May of 1872, Comanche Chief Long Horn led a band of his warriors into north Texas. Joining the raid were two Kiowa braves who were visiting his camp and were tempted by the idea of striking a blow against the settlers encroaching on their hunting grounds. On the 19th of that month, five of the Indians, including the two Kiowa, were separated from the main band and unexpectedly rode into a party of surveyors near Round Timbers, east of Fort Belknap. The surveyors were heavily armed and instantly engaged the Indians, firing rapidly. Soon they had driven the Indians into a ravine and trapped them in the brush at one end.

While the battle raged, one of the Comanche slipped through the woods and escaped. But his four companions were not as fortunate and fell under the deadly fire inflicted by the surveyors. The young brother of Kiowa War Chief White Horse was among the dead, and when the chief learned of his brother's death, he swore revenge. In early June, with his friend Chief Big Bow, Chief White Horse led a raid into Texas, promising not to return until Texans had been killed, or he had died avenging his brother's death.

Two months before this event, Abel and Millah Lee, along with four of their children, had moved from Jack County to the Clear Fork country. Not realizing they were on a collision course with death and destruction, they discovered and moved into the abandoned house of the Dobson family at the mouth of Kings Creek on the Clear Fork of the Brazos River, about sixteen miles east of Fort Griffin.

Now, a few weeks after the surveyors killed the Indian, on a warm Sunday morning, June 9, Abel Lee was sitting in his rocker on the front porch of his picket house, singing hymns in his fine clear voice. Occasionally he glanced through the front door, keeping an eye on a young man who was visiting his sixteen-year-old daughter, Susan. Suddenly, shots rang out: The Kiowa warriors had slipped up the bank in the brush along the river. Abel was taken completely by surprise and fell mortally wounded, shot through the chest. The Indians rushed to his body and scalped him entirely, removing all of the skin on his head that grew hair and then cut off both of his ears.

They charged into the house as the rest of the family—Mrs. Lee, her four children, and the young suitor—tried desperately to run. Mrs. Lee was shot in the back with an arrow and fell near the back door. As she lay there, she was scalped, her left arm was cut off and her body mutilated. The children fled the house looking for a place to hide, but fourteen-year-old Cordelia was overtaken near the cow pen. Hearing her screams, Susan stopped and came back to help, but she had no chance to save her sister and was herself taken captive. The Indians quickly scalped Cordelia and then turned their attention to finding the other children. Seven-year-old John and nine-year-old Millah Frances (Milly), ran into the cornfield behind the house and hid in the tall corn. The young man courting Susan kept running and got away. John and Milly, afraid and trembling as their hearts pounded in their chests, suffered agonizing minutes as the Indians searched the field. Finally they were discovered and rough hands grabbed them and dragged them back to the house.

After taking the three children captive, the Indians spent some time ransacking the house, ripping feather bedding and amusing themselves by putting on clothes they found. Susan was led through the house and forced to suffer the agony of seeing her mother's dismembered and bloody body as she still breathed but obviously was dying. Finally, mounting their horses and securing their captives, the Kiowa headed north to the Indian Territory. Susan was tied on a horse by herself, while Milly was put on behind a squaw, and John was placed behind a warrior.

The next day, the bodies of Mr. and Mrs. Lee and their daughter Cordelia were found by J. C. Irwin, Johnny Hazelett, and other Clear Fork settlers. They were buried on the north side of the house about fifteen paces from the back door. Word of the atrocity was sent to Fort Griffin, and Lieutenant E. C. Gilbreath with ten troopers and two Tonkawa Indian scouts were dispatched to investigate.

The soldiers left the post at 12:30 p.m. on June 10th and found the regular river crossing near the Tonkawa Indian village not fordable due to high water. They proceeded to the Jackson crossing one mile down river, but found it the same. They were compelled to go down river on the right bank even though the Lee house was on the left bank. Finding the creeks also swollen from the recent heavy rains, they were forced to take a circuitous route, marching nearly twenty-seven miles. Finally, at 7:00 p.m., Lieutenant Gilbreath arrived across the river from the Lee home. The river was still too high to cross at that point, but one of the troopers volunteered to try and almost drowned in the attempt. Lieutenant Gilbreath had to learn the details by shouting across the river to the people burying the dead. He was also told that the Indians had camped eight to fifteen miles from the house toward the head of Kings Creek the night after the murders.

With the help of Hank Smith, who was camped on the right bank, the cavalry managed to cross upriver. Following the creek, the Tonkawa scouts succeeded in locating the Indian camp from the night before. It was evident that the Indians had left camp early that morning and by then had a twenty-hour head start. Leaving Kings Creek at 4:00 a.m., the weary troopers, after twenty-one hours in the saddle, rode into Fort Griffin at 9:00 the morning of June 11th.

Determined to find the captives, the Lieutenant immediately sent word to Lawrie Tatum, the Indian agent, requesting him to search the different camps in the Indian Territory. Mr. Tatum diligently searched the Territory, and with the help of Chief Lone Wolf, located the Lee children in Chief White Horse's camp. In the past, white captives had been ransomed or traded from the Indians. Sometimes they were traded for horses, other times they paid from $100 to $1500 for their release.

This time, however, agent Tatum told Chief White Horse to turn the children over or he would summon the soldiers from Fort Griffin to take the children back by force. White Horse realized the agent was not bluffing, so the children were brought forward and released.

Mr. Tatum's resolve had, for the first time, influenced the return of captives without ransom. They were given a military escort back to Texas. The three young pioneers had physically survived their ordeal, but the mental anguish, including the terrible memories of seeing their father, mother, and sister slaughtered, lasted much longer—perhaps for as long as they lived. For now they could only try to rebuild their lives.

HISTORICAL NOTES:

There was one Indian woman with the raiding party at the Lee massacre, believed to be Big Bow's wife. In Lieutenant Gilbreath's report, he stated that all of them were scalped in such a way that every particle of skin upon which the hair grew was removed from the head.

Right and left river bank: When facing down stream, the right bank is on the right-hand side and the left bank is on the left-hand side.

Very little is known about the Lee children after they were returned, beyond the following information:

John Lee homesteaded property in 1905 in Estancia Valley, New Mexico. He was at that time thirty-three years old.

Susan Lee married J. Q. Marble on March 13, 1873, in Palo Pinto County. She was seventeen years old, and it was less than a year after the massacre of her family.

The author has not been able to confirm with finality what information is recorded about *Millah Frances Lee (Milly)* after she was rescued. Evidence suggests she lived out her life in Florida.

CHAPTER 13

BIRTH OF A GRAVEYARD

Many of the real gunmen and "bad men" of the frontier passed through Fort Griffin. Some stayed only a short time while others settled for several years. John Larn, one of the true gunmen and a man with no aversion to killing, arrived about 1870. He was hired in the fall of 1871 as the trail foreman for a Colorado cattle drive by Bill Hays, a well-known stockman at Fort Griffin.

John and his trail crew left with 400 head of cattle but arrived in Trinidad, Colorado, with 1700 head. Mr. Hays asked no questions about the increase and was pleased to receive the cattle. However, Hays' good luck soon ran out: The livestock market had dropped, and he was unable to get a good price for his stock. His men were demanding their wages, and he had to borrow money to pay them. Hoping for better prices the next spring, he decided to hold the herd in Colorado through the winter, Then, because it was branding time on his ranges in Texas and he was concerned about his business interests around Fort Griffin, he gave John Larn his power of attorney and instructed him to return to Texas to manage his cattle there while he was tending the Colorado herd.

By the summer of 1873, his creditors had taken over his herd in Colorado, and he rode back to Texas. As soon as he arrived in Fort Griffin, he inspected his cattle and discovered that John Larn had accumulated a substantial herd of his own in a short time. Being a man knowledgeable in how to increase a herd quickly, Hays was suspicious, and a heated argument soon erupted between the two men over some of the brands.

Bill Hays and his brother John were in need of money and decided to try another drive, this time to Fort Sill, Oklahoma. They hired six men as a trail crew. Some of the disputed cattle were gathered and included in the herd, which infuriated John Larn. He rode into Fort Griffin to see

Rily Carter, the acting sheriff, and swore out a warrant against the Hays outfit, charging them with cattle rustling.

The Hays boys and the men with them were tough characters, especially Bill Bush, who was known to be a deadly man with a gun. Sheriff Carter, a cautious man, requested assistance from Fort Griffin's post commander. Colonel W. H. Wood issued orders for Lieutenant Turner to take thirteen troopers of the Tenth Cavalry and help bring back the wanted men. Sheriff Carter, John Larn, and the cavalrymen immediately followed the trail of the herd heading north and quickly located the men they were hunting, about eighteen miles from Fort Griffin camped for the noon meal on Bush Knob Creek.

The Hays men had no intention of returning to Fort Griffin and, when the sheriff and soldiers appeared, gunfire exploded. Bill Bush, the most dangerous gunman, was shot first, and John and Bill Hays were killed where they stood. Two more of the cattlemen were also killed with the first volley, and the other three quickly surrendered. Surprisingly, none of the lawmen were hit by the flying bullets. After the dust settled, they discovered that one of the three captured was a fourteen-year-old boy, and he was released. On the return trip to Fort Griffin the other two accused cattle thieves tried to escape and were shot to death.

At Fort Griffin a man named Rice was employed to bury the seven dead men, and he enlisted the aid of Mrs. Hank Smith's brothers. They returned the two men killed on the trail to the noon camp and then buried all seven there. The burials ended another bloody chapter in the history of Fort Griffin and, incidentally, started another graveyard.

HISTORICAL NOTES:

The graves of the seven men were the first graves in the Bush Knob Cemetery that is still maintained and in use today. There were small round markers for the seven original graves, but they are now gone. The graves are located in the southwest corner of the cemetery.

At the time of this incident, the Hays' cow camp was on Elm Creek, now named Bush Knob Creek.

John Larn, leader of the posse, was arrested for cattle rustling and jailed in Albany just five years later, in June 1878. There he was shot and killed by local vigilantes.

Members of the Hays outfit that were killed included George Snow, John Hays, Bill Hays, Bill Bush, "Gov." Jeames, "Hardtimes" Jeames, and "Nosy" Wilson.

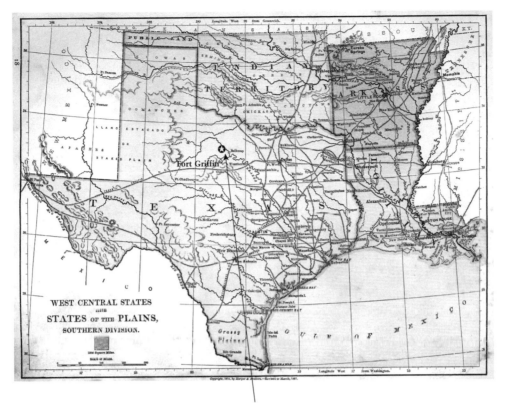

Fort Griffin

Bush Knob Cemetery

CHAPTER 14

THE WARREN WAGON TRAIN

There were several events that became turning points for the Comanche and Kiowa Indians in their attempt to rule the great Texas frontier and to protect the massive buffalo herds that provided their sustenance. One of the first events was the invention of the 1837 Colt Patterson revolver, as it increased the firepower of the settlers and Texas Rangers. Before that time, a Ranger carrying two pistols had two shots. With two of the new revolvers, however, ten shots could be fired before having to reload, resulting in a much more effective fighting force.

One of the last turning points occurred thirty-four years later in 1871, when the warriors of the plains almost killed the highest-ranking U.S. military officer. This event caused the military to accelerate the removal of the Indians from the Llano Estacado. The final turning point was the annihilation of the southern buffalo herd in Texas between 1874 and 1878, when hide hunters killed eight million buffalo, effectively closing the vast Texas frontier to the Indian.

In 1871, the country was recovering from the Civil War and trying to reestablish a military presence for the settlement of the frontier. In Washington, D.C., Chief of Staff William Tecumseh Sherman was receiving almost daily outcries from the westerners about full-scale depredations perpetrated by the Indians. He doubted the validity of these reports and considered them greatly exaggerated, but the settlers continued their pleas for him to end the carnage until he finally was prompted to go and see for himself.

He traveled from Washington, D.C., to San Antonio to begin an inspection tour of the Texas western frontier. General Sherman's entourage included his personal staff members and Inspector General R. B. Marcy, as well as an escort of seventeen cavalrymen handpicked from the Tenth

Cavalry. Leaving San Antonio early on the morning of April 28, they traveled by way of Fort McKavett and Fort Concho, finally arriving at Fort Griffin on May 15. They were not attacked by Indians and saw none in the two weeks of travel from San Antonio, so Sherman was still convinced the Indian depredations were not as bad as were being reported. General Marcy, however, could see that the frontier was much less populated than it had been on his trips several years before and realized the seriousness of the situation.

At Fort Griffin, General Sherman received a number of visitors who bombarded him with stories of capture, torture, and death at the hands of Indians and asked him to unleash his soldiers against this dreaded enemy. Before leaving, General Sherman visited First Lieutenant Fred Grant, son of President Ulysses S. Grant, and delivered a personal message from his father. From Fort Griffin, the two men traveled to the abandoned post of Fort Belknap and arrived at Fort Richardson on May 18, 1871.

Early the next morning, Thomas Brazeale and another teamster, both bloodstained and exhausted, staggered into the fort with a story of death and destruction. While the post surgeon treated the bullet wound in Thomas' foot, Thomas told General Sherman about the massacre. One hundred Indians had set up an ambush on the same road the general had traveled the day before. In fact, the Indians were there when Sherman and his party rode through. They had not attacked the soldiers because their medicine man Maman-Ti (Owl Prophet) had told the raiders he had seen this group in a vision. He felt that it should be allowed to pass because a second band of settlers and military were coming and could be attacked with better results.

Just hours ago, on an afternoon warm and sunny, the Henry Warren Wagon Train, with ten wagons freighting corn from Fort Richardson to Fort Griffin, arrived and, unsuspecting of any danger, rode into the trap. The Indians waited until the train was helplessly in their grasp and then suddenly attacked with violent fury. Thomas Brazeale, the lead driver, desperately tried to lead the wagons into a defensive circle. The Indians, having seen that maneuver before, killed one of the teams, not allowing the circle to be completed. The battle raged for a few minutes, but the teamsters, greatly outnumbered, were soon overcome.

In the confusion of swarming warriors, running horses, and flying bullets, five of the travelers managed to run the one hundred yards to the timberline and escape through the brush. The other seven were killed. Samuel Elliot was tied to a wagon pole and burned alive after his tongue had been cut out. The Indians were avenging the painful wound that Samuel had inflicted on their fellow warrior when he shot the warrior through the jaw. All were killed savagely, though. Another traveler's skull was split open with an axe, and all the rest were mutilated before dying. The Indian women on the top of a nearby hill cheered the attack, jumping up and down, yelling and clapping their hands.

Thomas Brazeale had fought off fear, exhaustion, and the pain of his wounds to make it to Fort Richardson. As General Sherman sat and listened to the bloody story, he realized it was only by a quirk of fate that he was still alive and had not been killed on that lonely, dusty road. Suddenly, the General had an entirely different evaluation of the extent of the Indian atrocities on the Texas frontier. He immediately issued orders to Colonel Randall Mackenzie from Fort Richardson and Major W. H. Wood from Fort Griffin to follow and capture the guilty Indians, posthaste. Mackenzie was on the march by noon with 150 troopers, while Captain Wirt Davis with Company F from the Fourth Cavalry plus several companies from the Tenth Cavalry took the field from Fort Griffin.

Arriving at the massacre site, Mackenzie ordered Sergeant Miles Varily to form a burial detail for the remains of the seven men. A large pit was dug, the bodies were put in a wagon bed and buried in a common grave. Seven marks were scratched in a large stone that was then placed at the head of the grave. Rain had begun falling earlier and continued through the next several days, obliterating the Indian trail. Colonel Mackenzie and Captain Davis were forced to trudge through mud as they searched for the fleeing Indians throughout north-central Texas and into Indian Territory (now Oklahoma).

General Sherman immediately left for the Indian Territory and upon arrival at Fort Sill met with Indian agent Lawrie Tatum to detail the Indian raid into Texas. A band of Kiowa rode into the Fort Sill Agency on May 27 to receive their monthly supplies, and agent Tatum summoned their leaders to his office and questioned them about the Texas raid. Chief Satanta rose, declaring, "Look here. Some of the other Indians will tell you they led the raid, but they are lying Indians. I planned it, and I led it. Satank, Big Tree, Eagle Heart, Fast Bear, and Big Bow were there, but I led it."

Agent Tatum quietly went to General Sherman and Colonel Grierson, Commander of Fort Sill, and related what he had been told. Plans were quickly made to capture the chiefs, and cavalrymen were ordered to saddle their horses and to take up positions around the fort to prevent escape. A dozen troopers were stationed inside Colonel Grierson's house behind shuttered windows. Word was sent to the chiefs requesting a meeting on the front porch of the Colonel's home. Chief Satanta was the first to arrive and, as he wanted to see the big chief from Washington, he readily admitted his part in the raid. When Satanta started to leave, Grierson drew his pistol and ordered him to sit down. After a slight hesitation, the chief obeyed. Within a few minutes, Satank arrived with twenty of his warriors. As he stepped up on the porch, he was told he was under arrest. He flew into a rage and grabbed for a pistol under his blankets. Immediately, the shuttered windows burst open, revealing a dozen soldiers with cocked and leveled rifles, and Satank subsided. The two chiefs were put in irons and taken to jail. From a distance, Big Bow and Eagle Heart witnessed the capture of their compatriots. They slipped out of the fort cunningly, eased through the mounted soldiers standing guard, and escaped.

Sherman and Grierson, stationed on the porch and alert to further developments, after a short time sighted Lone Wolf riding up from the post trader's, weaponed with two Spencer rifles, arrows, and a bow. As he approached, he tossed one rifle to a warrior, the bow to another, and dismounted to face General Sherman with a fully cocked rifle.

This moment was brittle with tension, for the slightest mistake would release a blood bath. Sherman, battle-tested, having faced fire many times during the Civil War, was able to act decisively to diffuse the situation. Seizing the death-dealing end of Lone Wolf's rifle to divert his aim, Sherman in even, steely tones told interpreter Horace Jones to say to the Indians that "no matter what happened or who was killed here today," the guilty chiefs would be taken back to Texas to stand trial. Lone Wolf stood rigid, his eyes spitting fire as he read the resolve of Sherman. Agonizing seconds slowly ticked by, each warrior testing the other's will through the rod of iron in their common grasp. Lone Wolf decided to lower the gun. He turned and walked away. He was allowed to leave the scene because he had not been named by Satanta, although he very well may have been on the raid.

General Sherman soon learned that Big Tree was at the post trader's store, so he sent a squad of troopers to arrest him. As the soldiers walked into the room, Big Tree realized something was wrong because these soldiers were looking directly at him. He sprinted down the room, pulled a blanket over his head, jumped through a glass window, and hit the ground running. Mounted troopers gave chase and soon had him surrounded; he was taken to jail with Satanta and Satank.

Colonel Mackenzie, who had been spending long hours in the saddle for over two weeks conducting an extensive search that yielded no results, finally led his troops into Fort Sill on June 4. To his surprise and delight, he found the guilty Indians had been captured and were in the guardhouse waiting to be transported back to Texas. He spent the next four days re-supplying and resting his troops, preparing for the return trip, and by June 8, he was ready. Wagons were brought to the jail for the prisoners, and Satanta and Big Tree calmly climbed in. But Satank, who belonged to a warrior society that was limited to the ten bravest warriors in the tribe, fought every step of the way. Satank was placed in another wagon with a heavily mounted guard, and the column began the journey to Jacksboro, where the trials were to take place.

Almost immediately, Satank began singing his death song. His hands were slender, and after gnawing the flesh off the thumb of one hand, he was able to slip out of his handcuffs. He then drew a knife from the folds of his blanket and stabbed a guard in the leg and grabbed his carbine. While he was bringing the gun up for a shot, Lieutenant George Alva Thurston quickly gave the order to commence firing, and the old chief went down, having taken several bullet wounds. Still, Satank sat up, and with superhuman strength, rose to his feet. He once again tried to bring the rifle into play, but the lieutenant ordered the troopers to fire. This time, after taking more hits, the warrior went down for good. Unfortunately, the teamster who was driving the wagon was also wounded, by friendly fire.

The procession moved on towards Jacksboro, leaving Satank's body beside the road for others to bury. Each night, Satanta and Big Tree were placed on their backs with their hands and feet tied to stakes driven into the ground. The soldiers were on the trail from Fort Sill for over a week and, as they neared Jacksboro, the two chiefs were mounted on mules, with their feet tied together under each mule's belly. Led through town to the military post, they were placed in the stone morgue that was to be their jail.

Twenty-two days later, on July 5, they were put on trial for their attack on the corn train and the murder of the seven teamsters. This was the first time Indians were tried in a court of law, and large crowds gathered for the spectacle. They were prosecuted by S. W. T. Landum, who later became governor of Texas, and defended by Thomas Ball and Joseph A. Woolfolk in two separate trials, both presided over by District Judge Charles P. Soward. Big Tree's trial was held first. After a day of testimony, the jury deliberated briefly and returned a guilty verdict of first-degree murder, assessing a sentence of death. The next morning, Satanta was led into the court room and jury selection began again, but this time only six new jurors that were acceptable to both sides could be found for Satanta. After some discussion there occurred a surprising twist to the trials: The jury from Big Tree's trial was sworn in, to sit in judgment of Satanta. After testimony was heard, Satanta stood up and, through interpreters, spoke on his own behalf saying, in part, that he was innocent and had not hurt any of his friends, the Tehannas (the settlers), but if he were allowed to go free, he would personally run down the dirty, lying, guilty Indians and kill them with his own hands. He then went on to say, "But if you kill me, it will be like a spark in the prairie; make big fire! Burn heap!" The verdict was predictable. The same jury, after a few minutes of deliberation, found him guilty of murder in the first degree with the punishment of death.

Trial Judge Charles Soward and Indian agent Lawrie Tatum knew that one of the inherent traits of these Indians was to seek revenge, so they believed that if the hangings were carried out on September 1 as scheduled, Satanta's words would come true—and the frontier would run red with blood. They successfully convinced Texas Governor Edmund J. Davis to commute the sentences to life imprisonment. The chiefs were transported by stagecoach to Huntsville and incarcerated in the state prison, but after spending only two years of their life sentence, they were paroled and returned to their people.

Big Tree adapted to a new way of life and did not continue to raid and plunder; he was even a Baptist Sunday School teacher when he died of old age. Satanta, on the other hand, remained a fierce warrior, and he was once again arrested for raiding and was returned to the state prison at Huntsville. He had spent his life free of boundaries and had roamed the vast western frontier as he pleased, taking pride in being a warrior and a leader of his people. The confined space of jail proved to be more than he could take, so he jumped from a second-story window, choosing to die rather than remain in prison.

HISTORICAL NOTES:

The corn train that was attacked is usually referred to as the Warren Wagon Train. However, it was actually owned by four partners: Henry Warren, J. C. DuBose, Ralph S. Mann, and Julian Fields.

The seven teamsters who were killed were N. J. Baxter, James S. Elliott, John Mullins, Nathaniel S. Long, Samuel Elliott, Jesse James Bowman, and James H. Wilson.

The five who survived were Charles Brady, R. A. Day, Hobbs Kerry, Dick Motor, and Thomas Brazeale.

Captain Wirt Davis and the Fourth Cavalry's Company F from Fort Griffin returned to the gravesite and erected a wooden monument listing the seven names of the slain teamsters.

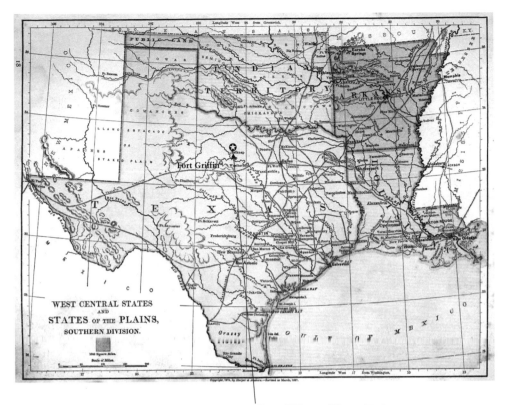

Site of Warren Wagon Train massacre

CHAPTER 15

TRUE STORIES FROM THE WESTERN FRONTIER

DINNER GUEST

On a cold day in October 1876, a buffalo hunter rode into Fort Griffin and sold several loads of flint hides, as the hunt that year had been successful. With the money in his pocket and trail dust in his throat, he headed for the nearest saloon. After several hours with a bottle of red-eye whiskey, the weight of hard miles and long hours began to lift; the more he drank the better he felt, and the better he felt the more he drank. By early evening he was feeling *r-e-a-l* good, and his thoughts turned to the fort on the hill and the blue-clad soldiers. Without a clear plan—or any plan at all—in mind, he headed up the hill to have a little fun at the soldiers' expense.

He had, after all, faced the wilds of the Texas frontier and survived, so surely he could handle a fort full of soldiers. It was the dinner hour, and he found the soldiers in the mess halls eating. As usual when in garrison, they were unarmed. The bold hunter stepped through the front door of mess hall number one, pulled two pistols from his belt, and began firing through the roof. Laughing and in a loud voice, he ordered the troopers to back out the door, to which they complied, and when the last one was out, he threatened to blow their heads off if they dared to return. The company captain was not amused and immediately ordered the lieutenant to form a squad of men, shoot the hunter, and retake the mess hall.

News of the incident rapidly spread to town, and upon hearing the story Sheriff John Larn hurried to the fort and tried to convince the captain he could talk the buffalo hunter into surrendering. Larn assured the captain he would take the shooter into custody, return him to town, and deal with him through the civil courts. After considering the situation, the captain gave him five minutes. Sheriff Larn walked up to the door, eased his head inside, and, after coaxing the drunk to put his guns down, marched his prisoner to town. There he was put in a small, one-room board-shack, and after finding a log to use as an anchor, the sheriff tied the door shut. It was a cold night, and the drunken hunter ripped boards out of the floor to build a fire. He ignited the old, dry lumber of the shack, which then went up like a tinderbox and was soon completely engulfed by flames.

By the time Sheriff Larn discovered the fire, the poor fellow was overcome by the heat and smoke. Fortunately, he was rescued before sustaining serious injuries. By the time he was dragged into the clear night air, he was stone cold sober, and the sheriff let him go on his way.

HISTORICAL NOTES:

After skinning the buffalo, the hides were pegged to the ground and allowed to dry. After drying, they were hard and stiff and were referred to as flint hides.

The cook in mess hall number one at Fort Griffin had the reputation of being the best cook on the frontier. Unfortunately, while at Fort Griffin, he experienced a nervous breakdown and spent the rest of his life in an asylum.

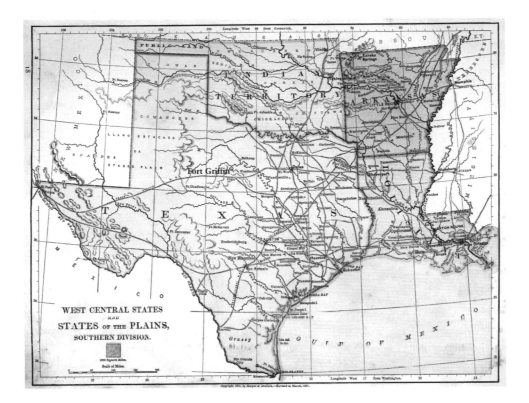

WEST CENTRAL STATES
AND
STATES OF THE PLAINS,
SOUTHERN DIVISION.

Scale of Miles.

CHAPTER 16

EARLY MORNING VISITORS

 band of Comanche led by two Mexican and Mulatto renegades soundlessly rode into the shadow of Fort Griffin on the night of March 4, 1868, to set up an ambush on Mill Creek, which was within two miles of the fort. At dawn on March 5, a government supply wagon train was returning to the fort, escorted by a small troop of the Sixth Cavalry. As they approached, they were instantly attacked by the Indians. Reacting quickly, the teamsters drove the wagons into a defensive position, and a heated battle erupted. In a flurry of activity, the cavalry escort returned fire while the teamsters unhitched the mule teams to prevent the wagons from moving while they were being used for protection. The small band of cavalrymen, some fresh from the battlefields of the Civil War, fought bravely, and the Indians soon decided to wait for a better day to take scalps. In the heat of the battle, however, the mules wandered away from the wagons, and the Indians quickly rounded them up and drove off with them.

Making their way on to the fort, the soldiers reported the incident to Lieutenant Colonel Samuel Sturgis about 7:30 that morning, who without delay summoned Captain Adna R. Chaffee. Captain Chaffee, a Civil War veteran, had just arrived at Fort Griffin a few days earlier to assume his duties in the Sixth Cavalry. Now he hurried to Colonel Sturgis' office and received orders to take sixty-two cavalry troopers and seven Tonkawa scouts and pursue the Comanche. Chafee's introduction to Texas came quickly, as he took the field for his first action in the great American West.

Chaffee assembled portions of Company I and Company E and easily picked up the fresh trail. The Tonkawa scouts set a fast pace and held to the trail as it continued south to the vicinity of the Ledbetter saltworks, which was located south and a little west of where Albany is today.

There the trail turned west, then northwest to Dead Man's Creek, crossing the Clear Fork of the Brazos River near the old, pre-Civil War outpost of Fort Phantom Hill. The soldiers had maintained a fast pace and were now closing in on the Indians. But the fleeing Comanche had outriders to the rear of the main band who spotted the approaching cavalrymen and reported this fact to their leader. The Indians immediately divided into two groups: The young braves took the stolen mules and headed west, while the seasoned warriors turned their horses northeast. Both bands kicked their horses into a run and easily pulled away from the troopers so that they were out of sight.

Captain Chaffee was faced with a decision. He did not want to divide his forces, and he very much wanted to punish the ones who had attacked the wagon train in the fort's backyard. So he led the contingent after the trail of the warriors, galloping all the way. It was late winter and the first week of March, and a cold "norther" blew in as the chase continued across the Texas frontier. The fleeing Comanche were trying to outdistance the troopers and lose themselves in the breaks of north-central Texas, but the cavalry followed as fast as the Tonkawa scouts could read the trail.

At daylight on the third day, the Tonkawa finally found the Comanche camp where they had sought protection from the cold, northern wind in the bottoms of the Wichita River. Chaffee quickly formulated a battle plan. Sending his scouts around the camp to cut off a retreat, he gave the order to draw pistols as he led a charge directly into the camp. The thundering charge of the cavalry, along with the bang, bang of their pistols and the war whoops of the Tonkawa caught the Indians completely by surprise. They had believed their mad dash over the last one hundred miles had lost the soldiers, and they were feeling safely hidden along the river.

Now they were in utter confusion. But as they were seasoned warriors, they recovered and put up a stubborn fight, desperately trying to break out of the grip of the determined troopers. With a final effort, a few managed to race through the brush and escape, but several of those who escaped were wounded. They left behind seven dead warriors, including the Mexican and Mulatto leaders.

All the Fort Griffin soldiers had survived the battle, yet three were wounded: Privates John F. Butler and Charles Huffman of Company I, and Private James Reagan of Company E. They had captured five Indian ponies, many bows and arrows, shields, and other camp equipment, and had succeeded in completely breaking up the camp.

Although weary from the long hours in the saddle and suffering from the cold, the troopers began the ride back to Fort Griffin feeling good about the success of the campaign. It had been nearly a year since they had arrived on the Texas frontier and established Fort Griffin, and until this fight they had experienced difficulty in locating and engaging the Comanche and their companions, the Kiowa. Many of these soldiers had fought in the Civil War and others had lived though European conflicts, but fighting the Texas Plains Indians was proving to be much different from those wars. These elusive warriors were the finest light cavalry they had ever encountered. But today's victory had been theirs, and they left the field of battle with a sense of satisfaction. Upon returning to the fort, Captain Chaffee reported to his commanding officer, who was very pleased with the results of his soldiers' efforts. On March 10, 1868, Colonel Sturgis issued Special Order No. 19, which said, in part:

> With the exception of the wounds of these men, the result is extremely gratifying, as was also the soldierly manner in which the troops bore their deprivations throughout the pursuit, suffering from the cold storm that raged throughout the entire march, without a murmur of discontent.
>
> In all campaigns where important results are achieved and especially against Indians, where the nature of the country is not well known, troops must expect to undergo hardships and deprivations, which cannot be foreseen or obviated; yet it is only the true soldiers who accept these inconveniences as necessary and unavoidable and who like men, maintain their spirit in spite of these.

HISTORICAL NOTE:

Adna Chaffee enlisted in the Sixth Cavalry on July 22, 1861, and was a member of that regiment for twenty-five years. He participated in the Civil War, the Indian Wars, and the Spanish–American War, and entered Peking in 1900 as a part of the China Relief Expedition.

CHAPTER 17

JUSTIFIABLE HOMICIDE

Charley Rath, seeking his fortune on the Texas frontier, drifted into Fort Griffin, working for a while as the post trader in partnership with F. E. Conrad. Charley later moved to the town of Fort Griffin and opened his own supply store in The Flat. But he is best remembered for "Rath City," a one-horse town he started as a buffalo supply town in 1876, just west of Fort Griffin. Six sod huts sprang up overnight; and before long there were two saloons, a laundry, two supply stores—the Reynolds' and Rath's—as well as two huts occupied as residences. The men and women who frequented this "prairie town" worked hard, fought hard, and drank hard. The town only lasted a short while, but, during its day, many weather-beaten cowboys and buffalo hunters rode down its one dusty street. As in most frontier towns, arguments and disagreements could quickly become deadly—and often did.

One sunny day in May 1877, several buffalo hunters had just come in from the killing fields and had been loafing around town, so just naturally they wandered into a saloon. One of the hunters, a man named Oleson, was refreshing himself in Aiken's Saloon and decided he was long overdue for a haircut. Not finding a barber in town, he turned to his fellow hunters for someone to trim his locks. Mr. Crawford, a good hunter and a fair hand with the skinning knife, rose to the occasion. Oleson seated himself in a straight-backed chair, and Crawford proceeded.

During the haircut, Tom Lumpkins strolled in and before long was making slighting remarks about an Indian battle the Rath City buffalo hunters had fought six weeks before. In early March, Comanche Indians had ambushed and killed Marshall Sewall while he was alone hunting buffalo. After burying him in a shallow grave dug with their skinning knives, his friends spread the alarm of impending danger from Indian attacks. Two days later, twenty hunters had gathered at Rath's, and soon the talk turned to retaliating against the Indians. Limpy Jim Smith, an ex-Montana outlaw, had been vocal with his opinion: They should organize and go after the Comanche. Tom Lumpkins had said, "Well, I have not lost any Indians, and I don't propose to find or hunt any." Limpy Jim had taken exception to his attitude, and heated words had been exchanged between the two men.

Now, trying to save face for declining to pursue the Indians with the other hunters, Tom Lumpkins continued to make light of their earlier efforts.

At first he was ignored, but he was not willing to let it drop, continuing to belittle the other hunters. Tempers were reaching the boiling point when suddenly, without warning, Tom drew his pistol and shot Mr. Oleson, breaking his arm close to the shoulder. Knowing his friend Oleson was unarmed, Crawford stepped between him and Lumpkins, trying to gain control of the situation before more blood was spilled. But Limpy Jim Smith, who was sitting to one side, jumped to his feet, pulled his revolver, and, pushing Crawford aside, returned fire. Tom, not expecting this development, backed out the door with Limpy Jim following—both blazing away with their six-shooters. Finally, Tom Lumpkins fell dead in the street, while the ex-Montana outlaw Limpy Jim sustained no wounds.

Another buffalo hunter named John Cook loaded the wounded Oleson in a wagon and took him to the post surgeon at Fort Griffin. The poor fellow endured the long, agonizing miles, bouncing along the wagon road with a broken arm. Limpy Jim Smith, asking several eyewitnesses to the shooting to accompany him, also went to Fort Griffin so as to surrender to the civil authorities of Shackelford County. His trial was held in April 1877 in Fort Griffin, and after deliberating a few minutes, the jury returned the verdict: "Justifiable homicide."

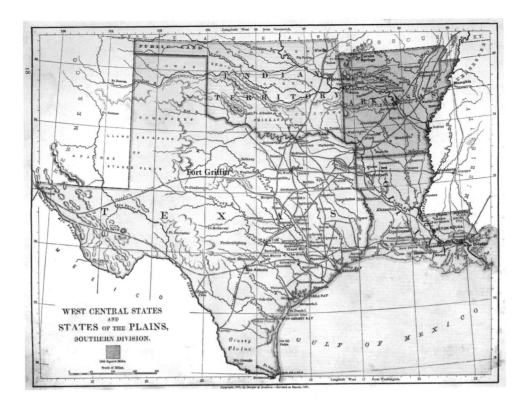

WEST CENTRAL STATES
AND
STATES OF THE PLAINS,
SOUTHERN DIVISION.

CHAPTER 18

HENRY MADE THE DIFFERENCE

ften a large raiding party of Indians riding into a section of the country they planned to attack would split into small groups and sweep the area, hitting different places simultaneously. They then would regroup at a prearranged meeting place before returning to their camp. On one such occasion, the Comanche came into the Clear Fork country near Fort Griffin and spread out along the river. At Bufford Creek they attacked and killed Joseph Brown. Several other settlers were in the same area and soon learned of the young man's death. Five of the men, including John R. and George B. Baylor, Elias Hale, Num Wright, and John Dawson, resolved to find the raiders, kill as many as possible, and run the rest out of the country.

John Baylor had been the first agent on the Comanche reservation at Camp Cooper, nine miles north of where Fort Griffin would be built, but he had been a long-time proponent of removing all Indians from Texas. He believed that "the only good Indians are the dead ones," and in 1859 led a strong settler force attempting to destroy the reservation. When the troops from Camp Cooper learned of Baylor's plans, they rallied to the reservation's aid and stopped the attack. However, the entire event did force the government to move the reservation Indians to Indian Territory (Oklahoma).

Baylor took charge of this small group and easily picked up the fresh trail and gave chase. Luck rode with them that day, and they located the Indians a few miles west of the site where the Reynolds brothers and Matthews family would build their ranch house on California Creek several years later in 1877. Concealing themselves in rocks and a thicket of live oak while they discussed a battle plan, they watched the Indians.

Baylor's men were armed with Henry repeating rifles, and it appeared the Indians possessed only bows and arrows. After observing the raiders for a while, they surmised that the Comanche were waiting for something or someone. Could this be the rendezvous point for other small groups of Indians that would be coming here also? If so, they needed to act swiftly before reinforcements arrived. Opening fire, the rapid action of the repeating rifles quickly dispatched all six of the Indians in this band. As soon as the fight was over, they concealed all evidence of the Indians and returned to their hiding place, settling down to await further developments. In less than an hour, eight more Comanche rode in, and the five sharpshooters repeated the same tactic, resulting in another victory. Throughout the day, five to ten Indians would arrive at a time and all met the same fate until nearly forty Indians had been killed. Finally, late that afternoon, a much larger group appeared, and the settlers were compelled to retreat and made good their escape.

Five men had dealt the most severe blow to a raiding party ever recorded along the Clear Fork of the Brazos River. Their repeating rifles had been the primary deciding factor, but their chances of success had also been greatly increased by finding cover in the heavy live oak thicket. Because the Comanche were always hesitant to rush an unseen foe for fear of an ambush, they had not put up a strong front on this day.

Baylor's group returned home heroes and was honored for bravery. At one barbecue, Mr. Baylor, in answer to praise, rose and said, "I and my men are all hard-shelled Baptists, and God Almighty goes with our sort." While John Baylor and men like him usually sought to take an offensive position, many of the other Clear Fork settlers took more of a defensive attitude and were willing to co-exist with the Indians when possible. The frontiersman had been victorious and won this battle, but there were many more battles to fight before this new country would be settled.

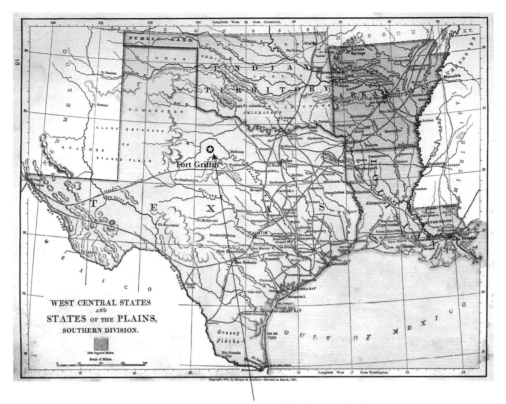

Site of Baylor's ambush

CHAPTER 19

EAST MEETS THE WEST

The year 1861 will forever be remembered as the time the devastating Civil War erupted and started the darkest days of our American heritage. That same year, George Washington Greer settled and built his home on the outer limits of the Texas frontier in what is now Shackelford County. Selecting a spot near Hubbard Creek, George quarried rocks from the stream and constructed his two-story house complete with a unique outside stairway to the second floor. Although Hubbard Creek was hundreds of miles removed from the great battlefields of the war, there was a heightened danger from Indian attacks because of its isolated location, so it was a real struggle to survive.

By 1867, the Civil War was two years over, and federal soldiers had returned to Texas to re-establish a western line of defense. Fort Griffin was built on the south side of the Clear Fork of the Brazos River, just twenty miles north of the Greer ranch. The Fort Griffin cavalry, especially in the early years, spent much of their time patrolling the frontier and performing escort duty for civilian and military travelers. In one instance, when the Fort Griffin paymaster was going to Fort Clark to receive the payroll, the major was provided an escort of ten troopers and one officer. Lieutenant Fred Grant, in charge of the guard, was the son of Ulysses S. Grant, president of the United States, and like his father would be promoted to the rank of general. Leaving the post at midmorning, they traveled to Hubbard Creek and camped at the crossing near George Greer's ranch.

Hospitality was a way of life, for these Texas settlers and travelers almost never were allowed to pass a home or a campfire without sharing a meal with the host. In this tradition, Uncle George invited all the soldiers to join his family for the evening meal, and, after mildly protesting, the entire troop marched to the Greer home. Mother Greer, learning there would be twelve visitors for supper, set about preparing the evening meal. Summoning several cowboys to help, she soon made the necessary adjustments and had enough food cooking on the fire. In short order, she had an appetizing meal of warm cornbread, coffee, fresh meat, and a big dish of fried potatoes. When the table was set and all was ready, George invited everyone to come in and be seated at the table.

The military in many aspects was very rigid and adhered to a very strict protocol. Officers and enlisted men would not dine at a common table. Lieutenant Grant, therefore, spoke up to say, "But Mr. Greer, the soldiers can wait until your family and the officers are served."

But Uncle George Greer had his own code of conduct, and in his home, his code ruled. He drew himself up, looked the lieutenant in the eye and replied, "Well, I'll be hornswoggled if they do!"

Trying to regain his composure, Lieutenant Grant persisted, "But the regulations of the army …"

"The regulations of your old *Yankee* army be hanged! See here, Mr. Lieutenant, if anybody waits for a second table, you dude officers can take a back seat and watch the balance eat!"

Embarrassed, Grant realized he was on friendly ground, and this was not a battle he wished to fight or an argument he wanted to pursue. The major, a veteran soldier trying to lighten the moment, said, "Come on, boys. We will go in and clean up the grub while the Lieutenant waits."

Lieutenant Grant laughed with everyone else. Then they all entered the house and seated themselves, and on this night officers and privates ate at the same table.

HISTORICAL NOTE:

Strict discipline and conduct protocol are absolute in the military, and rightly so: Lives are at stake on the battlefield. The best commanders do not disregard the rules, yet do have the ability to make quick decisions that produce the best results. Young Fred Grant demonstrated his command presence by adhering to his host's rules in his host's home, although it was a daring decision and could be considered controversial. This was a clash of cultures: military culture meeting frontier settler culture.

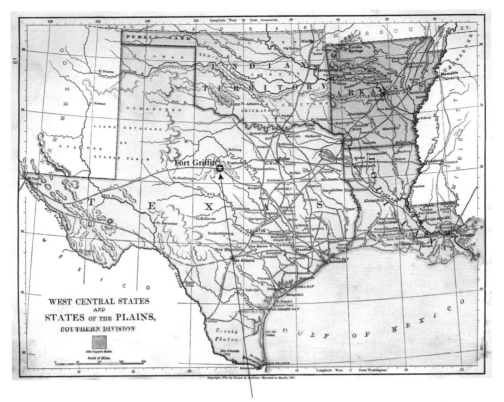

George Greer's ranch

85

CHAPTER 20

FRONTIER JUSTICE

Many of the soldiers at Fort Griffin were new to the frontier, and they had to adjust to the time and space of this big country. Arriving in Texas, these blue-clad warriors were overwhelmed by the enormity and fierceness of an endless frontier. They felt cut off and isolated from the rest of the world. But the grandeur of this vast new land was magnetic, and opportunities, like wild game, were plentiful. Many of the soldiers, after serving their tour of duty and leaving the army, stayed and became a part of the great Texas adventure.

On a clear fall morning, one such adventurer arrived at Fort Griffin. The fog was rising above the Clear Fork of the Brazos River as his troop of cavalry crossed the ford near the Tonkawa village and rode into the fort. Lieutenant Steele, a veteran of the Civil War, had been born in New Hampshire and had risen to the rank of colonel during the war, but, with the reorganization of the army after the war, he had been reduced to lieutenant. Serving out his enlistment at Fort Griffin, he and his wife then moved to The Flat, and "Colonel" Steele became one of its colorful characters.

He made friends easily and, being popular, was elected Justice of the Peace. During his tenure in that office, Colonel Steele enjoyed "socializing" in the many saloons with his friends, drinking and partaking in the games of chance. Often, the next morning he took the bench in his court with a black eye and swollen chin, but he had no aversion to fining his companions from the night before for being drunk and disorderly. Each man fined was surprised at his friend's sense of justice but had no recourse but to look astonished and mutter to himself.

Mike Kegan, a cowboy from the Sam Ward ranch, was a regular both in the saloons of The Flat and Judge Steele's court. One Saturday, Mike saddled his horse and, with his brother John, rode into Fort Griffin and tied up at Dick Jones' saloon. Mike was feeling wild and wooly and headed straight for the bar and a bottle of old red-eye whiskey. John was more conservative in his drinking and, as the afternoon wore on, and Mike became louder, he tried to intervene and temper his brother's fun. But Mike could only be restrained for so long. Finally, he leaped on his horse and charged up Griffin Avenue. Whooping the rebel yell, he fired his pistol, shooting at anything that snagged his attention.

Marshal Dave Barker, standing in front of the Clupp brothers' hardware store, saw him coming. Barker was a no-nonsense, lifetime lawman and, although cowboys were allowed to have fun on the streets of Fort Griffin, Mike Kegan was carrying it too far. Stepping into the hardware store, Dave picked up a double-barreled shotgun and a handful of shells. Loading both barrels with buckshot, he jumped into the middle of the street and leveled the shotgun on the charging cowboy. Mike realized he was in a dangerous spot and, as he slid his pony to a halt, he considered his chances in a gunfight with the marshal. At this range, the barrels of the shotgun looked like twin cannons, and Mike decided discretion was the better part of valor—and so surrendered.

Justice was swift as the marshal marched the corralled cowboy straight to Judge Steele's court. The county attorney wrote the complaint charging him with disturbing the peace, and the case was placed on the docket. It did not take Colonel Steele long to render his judgment: a five-dollar fine plus court costs. Mike handed him twenty-five dollars and, as he walked out the door said, "Keep the change for next time. I'm sure I'll be back before I leave town."

Mounting his pony, he loped back to the saloon, strolled inside and ordered whiskey. Mike's brother John arrived and appealed to Mike's reason, hoping he would now go home. Pushing his hat back, Mike studied his brother a moment, then suddenly reached and pulled John's pistol from his belt. He had come to town to be wild and wooly and was determined to make one more try for a successful charge down Main Street. He downed a shot of red-eye, walked to his horse, tightened his cinch, and stepped aboard. Firing his six-shooter, he touched spurs to his horse, and the dust boiled as he stormed back down the street, shooting with every jump.

Marshal Barker had expected Kegan to make another try, and when he heard the shots and thundering hooves, he immediately ran into the street ready for action. As soon as Mike was in range, Dave fired. The running horse flipped head over heels, and the rambunctious cowboy landed in a heap. Picking himself up and shaking off the dust, he found himself under arrest again—back to Judge Steele's court. Colonel Steele eyed the prisoner and asked, "Guilty, or not guilty?"

"Not guilty, your honor."

"Want a jury trial?"

"No, and I've already paid in advance."

Judge Steele leaned back in his chair and told the county attorney to present his case. The state called two witnesses who testified to the deed, and then closed. Judge Steele turned to Mike and asked whether he would like to call any witnesses. The cowboy looked amused and asked,

"Why would I want to call witnesses who saw the crime?" Colonel Steele once again reached a quick judgment: one hundred dollars plus court costs!

John was finally successful in convincing Mike to leave town, and the brothers rode back to the ranch, ready for another month of hard work.

Several years later, Mike Kegan's luck ran out, and he was killed in a shootout with other law enforcement officers.

Judge Steele remained in office until after the fort closed and the town began to vanish. Then, he also left, returning to Concord, New Hampshire. But, he was always grateful to the army for sending him to Fort Griffin and retained fond memories of the days he spent on the Clear Fork.

CHAPTER 21

FIRST CONFEDERATE AND INDIAN BATTLE

The stillness of the early morning hours of April 12, 1861, was shattered by the boom of the first shot fired at Fort Sumter, South Carolina, and this country was divided by the great Civil War. It was the dawn of the darkest four years in our history. The Second U.S. Cavalry, manning forts across the western Texas frontier, was withdrawn, and this new land was left unprotected. The frontiersmen living along the Clear Fork of the Brazos River, in what is now Shackelford County, were on the outer limits of the western edge and were perilously exposed.

The Texas Rangers were the state's forces and were left alone to protect the area from the Comanche and Kiowa. Unfortunately, they were vastly outnumbered and spread too far apart to be effective against the fierce, swift-riding Indians. Having joined the Confederate States of America, Texas sought assistance from the new Provisional Congress and was authorized two mounted regiments.

Captain Sayer arrived from Montgomery, Alabama, on May 7, 1861, and mustered the two regiments into the service of the Confederate States. He charged one regiment, The First Texas Mounted Rifles, with patrolling the western edge of the frontier from the Red River to the Rio Grande. The Indians, recognizing their opportunity to raid and plunder when the Second U.S. Cavalry left, were poised and ready to seize the moment.

Captain Buck Barry, commanding Company C, was assigned the northernmost section and established his headquarters at Camp Cooper on the Clear Fork River. He located Camp Jackson on the Red River at the confluence of the Wichita River, with camps at Willow Springs on the Little Wichita and on Fish Creek near the Brazos. He then devised a schedule of patrols that covered the area between each camp on a regular basis.

In July, Captain Barry received orders to provide a ten-man escort for a supply train going to the Red River station. Corporal Uracanbrack was placed in charge of the guard, and the detail left Camp Cooper early on a warm July morning. A week later, after a relatively easy trip and without encountering Indians, the train rolled into Camp Jackson. Taking the opportunity for a brief rest, the escort re-supplied and started the return trip to Camp Cooper. Reaching Willow Springs and still seeing no sign of Indians, they began to relax and enjoy the ride.

When they were crossing a stretch of open country eight miles south of the camp, they descried movement to their left, and suddenly a large band of Indians charged directly at them. They hesitated because it was difficult to form an immediate plan of action, for they were outnumbered forty-seven to ten and caught in the open without cover. Without help, their chances of survival were slim, and, at that moment, help seemed out of reach. There were soldiers back at Willow Springs, but that was eight long miles away, with very little cover. There were also a few troopers at Fish Creek, which was even farther away at fifteen miles, but that part of the trail did offer some cover. Apparently, the Indians realized the Confederate soldiers' dilemma and split into two squads, half of them racing to cut off retreat to the north, the others riding between the soldiers and Fish Creek. If there was to be a fighting chance, the soldiers had to act in a bold instant.

Knowing that cover was more important than the distance, the soldiers decided on Fish Creek. Drawing their weapons, the ten Confederate soldiers charged the southern line, which began a ten-mile running battle. Desperately, they rode to break through the Indians, but they were on tired horses and fighting well-mounted Comanche in five times their number. The wily Indians disbursed and regrouped at their front line, and the rear line moved up, bending along each side, drawing in tighter and tighter on the small band of Texans.

Again and again over the next ten miles, the soldiers broke through the line, only to be surrounded once more, with the Indians continually raining arrows down from all sides and yelling in triumph. With no hope of escape, the frontiersmen fought bravely, and three of their members were severely wounded. Once more they charged their tormentors, but their horses were exhausted and had very little speed left. As they hit the line once again, Private James McKnee was struck a fatal blow by a flying arrow and fell from his horse. Corporal Uracanbrack dashed to his rescue, jumped down from his horse, and tried to protect him from further injury. In the excitement, Uracanbrack's horse jerked free and ran through the Indians in the direction of the camp at Fish Creek.

Back at camp, the seven soldiers were surprised when the riderless horse ran into their picket line. The sergeant in charge reasoned that the escort must have been attacked by superior numbers and all had been killed, or there would have been a messenger instead of a lone horse. Finally, he decided to send a rider to Camp Cooper for more help, while the rest of the soldiers at the camp back-trailed the horse to learn the fates of their comrades. As they were mounting their horses, a rider came toward them from the distance; they called the runner back, and all seven rode to meet the haggard soldier. He told them that five were still alive, but at this very moment they were in the jaws of death, battling desperately for their lives and located three miles down the road. Racing their horses, rescuers flew over the miles— arriving on the field in a cloud of dust and so suddenly, that the Comanche thought their number to be larger than it was. They withdrew, leaving the battlefield to the Texans.

It was a ghastly sight that met the eyes the rescuers: death and destruction over a radius of a few feet with four dead horses, three seriously wounded soldiers and one soldier dying. It was dark by the time the four injured men could be moved to camp, after which two men were dispatched to Camp Cooper for a surgeon. The doctor arrived early the next morning accompanied by twenty-five soldiers. Sadly, Private McKnee had died during the night, but the wounds of the other three were treated, and they were evacuated to Camp Cooper, where they recovered and returned to active service.

Captain Barry took the field with thirty-two troopers, scouting for the Comanche. Three days later, on July 29, the troopers were attacked by seventy Indians just a few miles from where Corporal Uracanbrack and his men had made their previous stand. The Comanche attacked without warning. Privates Wetherby, Connelly, and Lynn were driving the pack mules some distance behind the main body of men and were killed instantly. Buck Barry, an astute tactician, did not hesitate to form his men into a line. They charged and routed the Indians, and a running, fifteen-mile fight ensued. A dozen Indians were killed, and finally, their apparent leader who wore an old U.S. Cavalry shell jacket went down. As soon as their leader fell, the hostiles dispersed in all directions, and the battle was over.

Dismounting lathered horses, the Confederate soldiers discovered that seven of their number had been wounded. The injured men were given first-aid treatment. They were hardy and healed quickly, and all recovered to fight another day. Turning their attention to a more solemn duty, they returned to their fallen comrades and, with hunting knives, dug one large grave. The three mule handlers were laid side by side and buried on the Texas prairie that they had defended. The soldiers carried rocks to pile on top of the grave to prevent its being dug into by wolves.

These seasoned frontiersmen spent the war years patrolling the vast Texas lands, and while they never fought any of the famous battles of the Civil War, they compiled an extensive record of their own bloody battles against the mighty Comanche and Kiowa Nations. In this first encounter, the soldiers had seen four men killed and ten wounded. Over the next four years, many more Confederate soldiers would shed blood and stain the Texas soil.

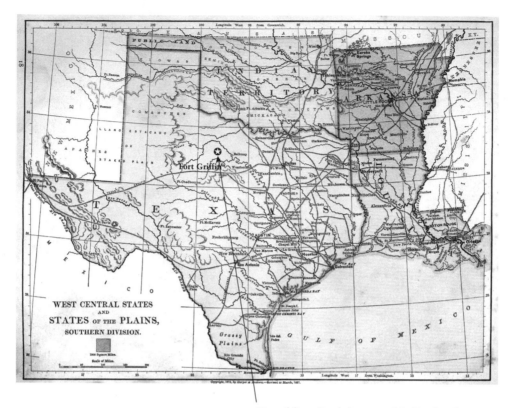

Site of first Confederate and Indian battle

PRIMARY SOURCES

THE LAST INDIAN FIGHT

1. Collinson, Frank. *Life in the Saddle*
2. Collins, John R. *The Border and the Buffalo*
3. *Fort Griffin Post Returns*, National Archives, Washington, D.C.

BEEHIVE SHOOTOUT

1. Interview with Watt Matthews
2. Site inspection by the author
3. *Fort Griffin Post Returns*, National Archives, Washington, D.C.
4. *Jacksboro Frontier Echo*, January 19, 1877
5. Hank C. Smith Papers, Panhandle Plains Historical Society
6. Correspondence, Newton Jones to J. R. Webb
7. Interviews with Joan Farmer
8. Grant, Ben O. *Early History of Shackelford County*, M.A. Thesis
9. Jeremiah M. Selman's Family Tree, compiled by William Beauchamp Selman
10. Matthews, Sallie Reynolds. *Interwoven*
11. Curry, W. Hubert. *Sun Rising on the West*
12. Robinson III, Charles. *Frontier World of Fort Griffin*
13. Hunter, J. Marvin. *The Story of Lottie Deno*
14. Rose, Cynthia. *Lottie Deno*
15. Metz, Leon C. *John Selman, Gunfighter*
16. Holden, Frances Mayhugh. *Lambshead Before Interwoven*
17. Historical Records of The Old Jail Art Center

ONE LONG NIGHT

1. Interviews with Watt Matthews
2. *Fort Griffin Post Returns*, National Archives, Washington, D.C.
3. Historical Records of The Old Jail Art Center
4. Interviews with Joan Farmer
5. Rye, Edgar. *The Quirt and the Spur*

MORNING DRINKS

1. Historical Records of The Old Jail Art Center
2. Interviews with Watt Matthews

3. Hunter, J. Marvin. *The Story of Lottie Deno*

4. Robinson III, Charles. *Frontier World of Fort Griffin*

A SURPRISE VISITOR

1. Metz, Leon C. *John Selman, Gunfighter*

2. Galbreath, Lester W. *Fort Griffin and the Clear Fork Country*

COMANCHE RAID, 1867

1. "Indian Fight on Double Mountain Fork of the Brazos: Wounding of Mr. G. T. Reynolds," early issue of *The Albany News*, Shackelford County, Texas, established 1883

2. Interviews with Watt Matthews

3. Matthews, Sallie Reynolds. *Interwoven*

4. Rye, Edgar. *The Quirt and the Spur*

5. Rister, Carl Coke. *Fort Griffin on the Texas Frontier*

ELM CREEK RAID

1. Historical tour and presentation by Bob Green

2. Historical records of Joan Farmer

3. Historical records of The Old Jail Art Center

4. Matthews, Sallie Reynolds. *Interwoven*

5. Ledbetter, Barbara Neal. *Fort Belknap: Frontier Saga*

6. Site inspections by the author

TWENTY TO ONE

1. Camp Cooper records of Margaret Putman

2. Simpson, Colonel Harold B. *Cry Comanche*

WHISTLING SAM

1. Interviews with Watt Matthews

2. Matthews, Sallie Reynolds. *Interwoven*

CHIEF OF RED MUD

1. Curry, W. Hubert. *Sun Rising on the West*

2. Rye, Edgar. *The Quirt and the Spur*

THE PRICE OF TOBACCO

1. *Fort Griffin Post Returns*, National Archives, Washington, D.C.

LEE FAMILY MASSACRE

1. Curry, W. Hubert. *Sun Rising on the West*
2. Correspondence with Wayland Ashmore, great-great-grandson of Able Lee
3. McConnell, Joseph Carroll. *The West Texas Frontier*
4. Ledbetter, Barbara Neal. *Fort Belknap: Frontier Saga*
5. Richardson, Rupert. *Frontier of Northwest Texas*
6. Mayhall, Mildred. "The Civilization of the American Indian Series." Vol. 63
7. Augar, Brigadier General C. C. "Army and Navy Journal." September 7, 1872
8. *Fort Griffin Post Returns,* National Archives, Washington, D.C.
9. Official Report written by Lieutenant Gilbreath, June 11, 1872

BIRTH OF A GRAVEYARD

1. Historical tour and presentation by Bob Green
2. Comstock, Henry Griswold. *Some of my Experiences and Observations of the South Plains during the Summer of 1871 and 1872: Memoirs of Henry Griswold Comstock*
3. John Chadbourne Irwin Memoirs
4. Site inspection by the author
5. Writings by Phin Reynolds
6. Blanton, Joseph Edwin. *John Larn*
7. Holden, Frances Mayhugh. *Lambshead Before Interwoven*
8. Metz, Leon C. *John Selman, Gunfighter*
9. Curry, W. Hubert. *Sun Rising on the West*
10. Galbreath, Lester W. *Fort Griffin and the Clear Fork Country*

WARREN WAGON TRAIN

1. Historical presentation by Bob Green
2. *Fort Griffin Post Returns,* National Archives, Washington, D.C.
3. Historical Records of Joan Farmer
4. Discussion with historian Barbara Neal Ledbetter
5. Comstock, Henry Griswold. *Some of my Experiences and Observations of the South Plains during the Summer of 1871 and 1872: Memoirs of Henry Griswold Comstock*
6. Matthews, Sallie Reynolds. *Interwoven*
7. Lechie, William H. *The Buffalo Soldiers*
8. Ledbetter, Barbara Neal. *Indian Raids*

DINNER GUEST

1. Grant, Ben O. *Early History of Shackelford County*, M.A. Thesis
2. Robinson III, Charles. *Frontier World of Fort Griffin*
3. *Fort Griffin Post Returns*, National Archives, Washington, D.C.

EARLY MORNING GUEST

1. Annual Report for 1868, U.S. Military: Department of Texas
2. General Orders, Fort Griffin, Texas
3. Rister, Carl Coke. *Fort Griffin on the Texas Frontier*

JUSTIFIABLE HOMICIDE

1. Cook, John R. *The Border and The Buffalo*
2. Rister, Carl Coke. *Fort Griffin on the Texas Frontier*

HENRY MADE THE DIFFERENCE

1. Rye, Edgar. *The Quirt and the Spur*
2. Matthews, Sallie Reynolds. *Interwoven*
3. Rister, Carl Coke. *Fort Griffin on the Texas Frontier*

EAST MEETS THE WEST

1. Rye, Edgar. *The Quirt and the Spur*

FRONTIER JUSTICE

1. Rye, Edgar. *The Quirt and the Spur*
2. *Fort Griffin Post Returns*, National Archives, Washington, D.C.
3. Historical Records of The Old Jail Art Center
4. Ledbetter, Barbara Neal. *Fort Belknap: Frontier Saga*

FIRST CONFEDERATE AND INDIAN BATTLE

1. Barry, Buck. *Buck Barry Texas Ranger and Frontiersman*
2. Smith, David Paul. *Frontier Defense in the Civil War: Texas Rangers and Rebels*
3. "Dallas News," First-person account by Frank Wristen
4. Special Orders, Number 40, June 18, 1861

INDEX